"I'm t
Rhea.

"I want to leave here, Joey. I want to take Nicci and leave Chicago."

He stopped, turned. "No."

"Damn you, Joey!"

"I may not have your respect right now, but I'll have your loyalty. You're stuck between a hard place and an even harder man, darlin'. Your future, and our son's, are mine. The sooner you get used to that, the better off you're going to be."

Rhea shook her head, her eyes wide. "What are you saying?"

"I'm saying that in three days, you're going to stand beside me...as my wife."

Dear Reader,

"In like a lion, out like a lamb." That's what they say about March, right? Well, there are no meek and mild lambs among this month's Intimate Moments heroines, that's for sure! In *Saving Dr. Ryan*, Karen Templeton begins a new miniseries, THE MEN OF MAYES COUNTY, while telling the story of a roadside delivery—yes, the baby kind—that leads to an improbable romance. Maddie Kincaid starts out looking like the one who needs saving, but it's really Dr. Ryan Logan who's in need of rescue.

We continue our trio of FAMILY SECRETS prequels with *The Phoenix Encounter* by Linda Castillo. Follow the secret-agent hero deep under cover—and watch as he rediscovers a love he'd thought was dead. But where do they go from there? Nina Bruhns tells a story of repentance, forgiveness and passion in *Sins of the Father*, while Eileen Wilks offers up tangled family ties and a seemingly insoluble dilemma in *Midnight Choices*. For Wendy Rosnau's heroine, there's only *One Way Out* as she chooses between being her lover's mistress—or his wife. Finally, Jenna Mills' heroine becomes *The Perfect Target*. She meets the seemingly perfect man, then has to decide whether he represents safety—or danger.

The excitement never flags—and there will be more next month, too. So don't miss a single Silhouette Intimate Moments title, because this is the line where you'll find the best and most exciting romance reading around.

Enjoy!

Leslie J. Wainger
Executive Senior Editor

Please address questions and book requests to:
Silhouette Reader Service
U.S.: 3010 Walden Ave., P.O. Box 1325, Buffalo, NY 14269
Canadian: P.O. Box 609, Fort Erie, Ont. L2A 5X3

One Way Out
WENDY ROSNAU

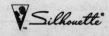

INTIMATE MOMENTS™

Published by Silhouette Books

America's Publisher of Contemporary Romance

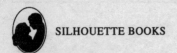 SILHOUETTE BOOKS

ISBN 0-373-27281-2

ONE WAY OUT

Copyright © 2003 by Wendy Rosnau

Visit Silhouette at www.eHarlequin.com

Printed in U.S.A.

WENDY ROSNAU

resides on sixty secluded acres in Minnesota with her husband and their six children. She now divides her time between her family-owned bookstore and writing romantic suspense.

Her first book, *The Long Hot Summer,* was a *Romantic Times* nominee for Best First Series Romance of 2000. Her third book, *The Right Side of the Law*, was a *Romantic Times* Top Pick. She received the Midwest Fiction Writers 2001 Rising Star Award.

Wendy loves to hear from her readers. Visit her Web site at www.wendyrosnau.com.

This book is dedicated to you, the readers,
who have expressed interest in my *Brotherhood* series
and the Masado brothers.

A special thanks to my editor, Gail Chasan,
for believing in me and for putting up
with my red ink pen time and again.
Also for allowing me the freedom needed
to make this series come alive on the page.

Grazie...

Chapter 1

At midnight Grace Palazzo suffered her second stroke of the year. Her struggle had been traumatic, but not fatal. It had sent the household into a panic and Rhea, along with Grace's daughter, into tears. But it wasn't the most significant drama to unfold on that stormy night on the third of November.

No, the real drama, at least for Rhea Williams, had come hours later when she had returned to her bedroom to find the silver cross glistening on her pillow.

She had scarcely been able to breathe as she backed out the door, then raced down the hall to Nicci's room. Only, she knew before she swung the door wide that her son was gone—that like a thief in the night, his father had breached the house and taken him.

She had prayed she was wrong, had prayed for mercy—a shred of compassion. But there was no mercy, no compassion, only an open window and an empty bed where her son had slept for the past two years.

A gust of wind lifted the curtain at her bedroom window, and in spite of the heat, Rhea shivered. Key West was warm, but after the sun went down, the wind could become as dangerous and unpredictable as a vengeful witch. Especially during hurricane season.

The smell of rain was heavy in the air, the pounding surf a constant roaring in her ears. The tropical storm the islanders had been preparing for was less than ten hours away. Rhea hated storms, but she would rather meet a hurricane head-on than return to Chicago and face Nicci's father.

In the beginning, all she had wanted was to go back, and for Joey to know about his son. But then the days had turned into months, the months into years, and slowly Santa Palazzo had become her home.

Oh God...he knew they had created a child—a beautiful black-haired, brown-eyed baby boy.

"What will you do, Rhea?"

The voice was soft behind her, as soft as the touch on her shoulder. Rhea turned from her bedroom window to face Grace's twenty-four-year-old daughter. Elena stood hugging herself, her eyes red from crying. Tonight had been a nightmare for both of them.

"Rhea, did you hear me? How will you get Nicci back?" When Rhea didn't answer right away, Elena squeezed her shoulder. "You're scaring me, Rhea. There's a way to get him back, isn't there? You'll fight, right?"

Fight Joey…

Elena had no idea how ridiculous that statement was. She had no idea what lay hidden behind all the closed doors to the past. She had no idea the complexity of the situation, or the danger. But then, why would she? She'd been carefully sheltered from the secrets by layers of lies—twenty-four years of lies.

"When I called to tell my father about Mom's stroke, we had no idea that Nicci had been kidnapped. But he's coming, Rhea. On his way right now. He'll be here in a few hours. We'll tell him what happened, and he'll know what to do. He loves Nicci. You know that."

Yes, she knew that. Frank thought the world of Nicci. That wasn't up for debate. What was, however, was how to defuse the time bomb that had started ticking the minute Joey had learned he had a son. And that's what would be foremost on Frank's mind when he learned Nicci had been taken by Joey.

But how could she tell Elena any of that, without explaining the rest? Without telling her that her father, Frank Palazzo, resident of Key West, Florida, was also Frank Masado, a member of the *famiglia* in the Chicago-Italian mafia. And if she went that far to disclose his double identity, she would have to tell

Elena all of it. She would have to confess that Frank was Nicci's grandfather.

Elena believed she was an only child. She had no idea that she was the half sister to Joey and Tomas Masado. She had no idea that her father had been previously married, or that he'd been juggling two separate lives with well-crafted scenarios and tightly woven lies to keep them all safe.

When Frank had brought Rhea to Key West three years ago, he had told Elena that he'd hired a live-in nurse for Grace. And that's how Rhea had been disguised—how the household at Santa Palazzo had come to accept her.

Grace's health over the years had gradually gotten worse, and she needed constant care. Rhea had been a nurse in Chicago for seven years. The situation had worked on all levels.

"Talk to me, Rhea. What can I do to help?"

"I don't want your mother to know what's happened. She's too fragile. She needs bed rest and no excitement for at least forty-eight hours. And your father…when he learns what happened tonight he'll know why I had to…"

"Leave. You are, aren't you."

"I can't wait, Elena. I'll go crazy waiting for your father to get here."

Elena reached out and tugged Rhea to the bed. Pulling her down to sit next to her, she said, "Mother would have died tonight if you hadn't been here to help her. If you leave, she'll have no one."

Rhea pushed her long blond bangs out of her eyes. "You're wonderful with your mother, Elena. You are why your mother has survived all these years. You and your father. She'll be fine until Frank comes. He'll order a replacement nurse within twenty-four hours."

"Why can't we just call the police and tell them that Nicci's been kidnapped? Tell them that you know who did it, and—"

"I can't do that," Rhea said quickly. "Nicci's father is a powerful man in Chicago. When I left I didn't tell him I was pregnant. I didn't say where I was going, either. I just left. I had my reasons. Good reasons. But..."

"I was always curious about Nicci's father," Elena admitted. "Is that where he gets his black hair and dark eyes? Does his father have black hair? You're so fair, and Nicci's so dark."

"Joey's Sicilian. His family..." Rhea glanced at Elena's dark hair, then her earthy brown eyes, "they all have black hair and dark eyes."

"Did you run away because he hurt you, Rhea? Was it Nicci's father who gave you the scars?"

Rhea saw Elena focus on the thin white line on her lower lip, then on the one that slipped into the corner of her left eye—the scar that had made her wear an eye patch for months. The scar that had nearly blinded her.

"It wasn't like that. Joey never hurt me."

Elena frowned. "Then, I don't understand."

"I was in an accident." Rhea shivered, remembering Stud's angry eyes as he'd picked her up and hurled her through her bedroom window. Her ex-husband had claimed he hadn't meant to hurt her, just to knock some sense into her. Elena didn't need to know the sordid details of Rhea's past, however, or the dangers that threatened her once she returned to Chicago. And likewise, Rhea didn't want to dwell on her ex-husband…or Joey.

Especially not Joey.

There was no rational explanation for falling in love with him three years ago. It had been one of those crazy chance meetings at a time when she should have been too wary of any man to notice the black-haired Sicilian in the hospital corridor during one of her unscheduled late-night visits.

At the time, she didn't know what caught her attention first, the meticulous way he dressed or his shockingly deep voice. Later, she came to realize it was neither. What had drawn her to Joey Masado was the hidden tenderness in the depth of his dark eyes despite his poignant tough-guy image—a goodness and a fairness that defied reason, as well as rumor.

"How soon are you leaving?"

The thought of returning to Chicago scared Rhea. But she forced a weak smile. "As soon as I can book a flight. While I pack, will you call the airport? I need to get out of here before the storm hits and they start grounding planes."

And before Frank comes home and tries to stop me.
"Will you come back?"

"Yes. I'll be back. With Nicci." Rhea knew that it was the only way to defuse the time bomb—if she and Nicci returned to Santa Palazzo. How she was going to manage that wasn't clear just yet, but she would focus on that once she had faced Joey and knew that Nicci was all right.

Elena shoved her long black hair away from her face, and stood. "I'll call the airport." She headed for the door, then turned back. "I love you and Nicci. I know I've never told you that, Rhea. But it's true. I can't imagine either of you not in my life."

The uncertainty of the situation brought tears to Rhea's eyes, and she came off the bed quickly. "I love you, too. I've always wanted a sister, and you've been that to me. Thank you for accepting me into your home, Elena."

"Oh, Rhea." Suddenly Elena rushed back and threw herself into Rhea's arms. "If you need me, I'm here. Don't forget that. Don't forget me."

The drive to the airport was hampered by heavy rain. When Rhea boarded the plane it was in a down-pour, the wind so savage that she was glad she had worn jeans and her brown suede jacket.

When the plane was finally airborne, she pulled the silver cross from her pocket and stared down at it. Unbidden, the image of Joey, half naked, wearing the silver cross nestled against the black hair on his chest materialized, and with it a fierce longing that had her feeling anxious as well as frightened.

Three years hadn't dimmed his powerful image or the emotions that had kept the memories alive. If anything, the years had sharpened the picture in her mind's eye, and strengthened her belief that for a brief moment in time she had experienced heaven on earth.

It rained throughout the night. All the way through Florida and Georgia. Hours later, Rhea changed flights in Nashville, and as she watched the dawn of a new day from her seat among the clouds, a small private aircraft made its final descent onto a runway at Chicago's O'Hare International. And like the tough Sicilian heritage Niccolo Joseph Masado had been born into, the black-haired two-year-old boy asleep in his father's arms never fussed or blinked an eye as his uncle Tomas landed the sleek white Cessna in a rush of speed, tires squealing on black tarmac.

As choices went, this one had been easy. There had been risks involved, but then, Joey Masado was used to taking risks. He was a suit-and-tie business-man, considered the best moneyman in Chicago. But tonight, unshaven, wearing jeans and a sweater, he'd been simply a father on a mission to claim what was rightfully his.

Joey reached out and straightened the blanket that

covered his sleeping son. He was smaller than he'd expected. He couldn't help but worry about that. What if the boy was ill, or had been born sickly?

When he'd learned he had a son—a son he hadn't known existed until his brother had waltzed into his office three days ago and slapped the proof down on his desk—he hadn't believed it was possible. But the proof was no longer just a glossy photo, a flat image of a black-haired little boy walking on the beach hand-in-hand with his mother. The boy was flesh and blood.

His flesh and blood.

If the boy's mother had been anyone other than Rhea Williams, Joey would have refused to believe the child was his. He had always been careful when he'd climbed into a woman's bed. He'd never lost his head or forgotten himself. That is, not until he'd laid eyes on the sexy blond with the sad blue eyes.

No, Niccolo was definitely his son. He was as certain of that as he was of why Rhea had run away from Chicago three years ago. He had always thought she had vanished out of fear of her ex-husband. But now he knew that wasn't the case. Pregnant with his child—a Masado child—she had run to escape him and what their son would surely become if she stayed.

As hard as it was to accept, the proof was asleep in front of him—the proof of Rhea's betrayal.

"He looks just like the pictures of you hanging on the wall in the old house. I remember thinking that, the day I photographed him on the beach with Rhea.''

''That's what Jacky said, too. The picture, I mean.'' Joey turned to his brother, who stood in the doorway leaning heavily into the jamb. ''Jacky just left. But for the past hour, he's been sitting here staring at Niccolo and shaking his head.''

''The likeness is amazing,'' Tomas agreed.

Joey studied his brother. Tomas's eyes were bloodshot, which meant his back pain was giving him hell again, which meant he'd been drinking to compensate. He hated to see his brother drinking so much. He'd survived a serious beating a few months earlier. Hospitalized, he'd lost a kidney in his fight to survive. He had been cheating death since he was fourteen, a streak that had earned Tomas the nickname Nine-Lives-Lucky. Eventually it had been shortened to just Lucky.

Joey glanced back at Niccolo. ''I never realized how small a two-year-old is. He looked bigger in the picture.''

Lucky grinned. ''He's going to take some work. You up for that, or do you want to take him back, *fratello*? Have you changed your mind?''

Joey admitted he didn't know the first thing about raising his son, but the boy was his. That's all he'd been thinking about for three days. And all he'd had on his mind when they had slipped into Santa Palazzo under the cover of darkness.

His brother had told him in the plane that he would

back him in whatever decision he made concerning Niccolo. He'd said, "I'll be behind you or in front of you. Walking in the front door, or going in through a window. Two of the guards on the estate are mine. I put them in place before I flew back here. We should be able to enter the grounds without any trouble. Then again, if you want to make trouble, I brought along the *lupara. Capiche?*"

They hadn't used the sawed-off Italian shotgun. They'd gone in quietly through an open window off a balcony on the second floor. They were going in after his son, not to start a war. He hadn't wanted to frighten Niccolo or endanger him by flying bullets.

It had only taken a few minutes to locate his son's bedroom. Rhea's room, too, though he hadn't found her inside. His window of opportunity had been tight. They had ten minutes max to get in and back out. That's why he had left behind the cross on Rhea's pillow. If she cared at all about their son, he knew the cross would bring her back to Chicago.

"I need to hire a live-in nanny. Can you help me arrange some interviews tomorrow?"

"I'll get on it first thing. If we leave him alone, you think he'll be all right? We need to talk."

Joey looked down at his son. "He's finally sleeping, but he keeps asking for his bear."

"There's a kids' store in the lobby, I'll see what I can find. Are you ready to listen to what I have to say?"

"I was ready three days ago. You're the one who wanted to wait until after Niccolo was here."

"I didn't want what I had to tell you to interfere with what was most important."

"Meaning my decision to claim my son?"

"He's yours." Lucky hung his scarred hand on his jeans-clad hip. "If I had a son, I would want him with me."

"I'm ready for whatever comes at me," Joey told him. "I'll fight the devil, or anyone else who tries to come between me and what is mine."

"He's a good-looking boy, *fratello*. Worth fighting for. Come, let's talk and make some plans."

Joey's gaze went to his son. "I'll leave the door open and the hall light on. If he wakes up in the dark and starts crying, I don't know what I'll do."

"Guess you'll get your chance to play daddy. Rub his back and tell him a story."

Joey glanced at Lucky, then scowled when he saw his brother wearing an amused grin. "I don't know any stories."

"Sure you do. Remember the one Vina used to tell us? The one about the purple badass dragon who turned out to be a nice guy?"

Lavina Ward was their best friend's mother. As young boys they'd spent countless hours with Jackson and Lavina Ward. They had adopted Vina as the mother they never had, and Jackson as the once-in-a-lifetime friend who hadn't cared one bit what their name was, or what their father did for a living.

Twenty-eight years later, nothing had changed. Lavina was still baking *her boys* apple pies and buying them birthday presents. And Jackson, recently promoted as head of the CPD Special Investigations Unit, was still their best friend.

Joey tucked the blanket under his son's chin, then followed his brother to the living room. When Lucky made a detour and slipped behind the bar, Joey said, "I thought you were going to give up the booze. Or, at least, back off a little."

"I've rethought that. The way I see it, what's the difference if I get addicted to painkillers or scotch? You might need a stiff one yourself once you hear what I have to tell you."

Joey eased himself down on the red damask sofa that snaked around a massive Italian-marble coffee table.

Forty-nine stories up, Joey's penthouse covered the entire top floor of Masado Towers. The ceilings were eighteen-feet high, and the furniture was plush and oversize in shades of Italian bloodred and gold. The long bar was imported cherry wood. A collection of large mirrors surrounding it and throughout the apartment opened up the already extravagant space, as did the floor-to-ceiling windows that overlooked Grant Park and Lake Michigan.

Like the living area, the kitchen was a sprawling wonder filled with the latest conveniences and a number of skylights. A breakfast nook to the left of the kitchen offered a view of the city at sunrise, and the elegant dining room that jutted outward like a glass egg to the right, allowed for a breathtaking sunset view and a spectacular skylight panorama after dark.

When Lucky joined his brother, he brought Joey a glass of scotch and placed it on the coffee table. As he made himself comfortable on a gold tapestry chair, he said, "Trust me, you're going to need that."

"So, tell me what you know. Santa Palazzo was swarming with guards tonight. Whose place is it, and why so many guards?"

"The estate is never without guards. I've learned they're a permanent, round-the-clock fixture. No less then eight at all times."

"The electronic gates were high-tech. Some of the guards had dogs."

"Four dogs. Dobermans with an attitude." Lucky rubbed his thigh, indicating he'd had a conversation with one of them. "Before I tell you more about Santa Palazzo, I'll explain how I found the place. It all started with the packages."

"The packages?"

"For several years I've been mailing a package to a post office box in Key West every month. A job assigned to me eleven years ago when I was twenty. Since the packages were from various dress shops, I assumed they were gifts for one of Frank's lady friends. From time to time I would joke with him about his dedication to one woman, and when I did, Frank would smile and get this strange look on his face. Anyway, when Sunni Blais opened Silks here at Masado Towers, Frank started ordering the packages from her shop. Last month, when I went to Silks to pick up the monthly package, I took a minute to talk to Sunni. She and I had never exchanged more than a few words since she'd opened her shop. But this time was different.''

''Because Jacky was in town.''

Lucky nodded. ''He was living in her apartment. Acting as her bodyguard. But like you, I knew there was more between them.''

''So you were checking her out to see if she was right for Jacky.''

''We both know that women who look as good as Sunni does are usually bitches. But as it turned out, she was the exception to the rule. She's for real in every way.''

''We're in agreement on that. Tell me more about the packages,'' Joey pressed.

''During the conversation, Sunni said something I thought was odd. She said the two gifts inside the package were exactly what Frank had ordered this time. One in each size.''

''One in each size?''

''That's right. Two gifts. One in each size. For eleven years I thought I was picking up one gift for Frank's mistress. A mistress he obviously cared a lot about because he never missed a month. But suddenly I learned there were two gifts inside one package. And they were in different sizes.'' Lucky took a swallow of scotch. "I thought that was worth checking out, so I decided to fly down to Florida and stake out the post office box."

"And that led you to Santa Palazzo."

Lucky nodded. "For two days the same man showed up at the post office to retrieve the mail from the box. On the second day, I followed him. When he entered Santa Palazzo, and it was guarded like a fortress, my curiosity doubled. I decided to buy a camera and hang around for a few days to take some pictures. I wanted to see who came and went. That's when I discovered Rhea."

Lucky reached into his jacket pocket, pulled out a handful of pictures and tossed them on the coffee table. "I figure you know where this is going. Those are the people who went in and out, the four days I watched the house. There's only one in there that you'll recognize other than Rhea."

Joey reached for the pictures and shuffled through them, looking for confirmation of what he already knew. When he spied the picture, he said, "Frank was there. He's known where Rhea's been hiding the entire time."

"It looks that way. But there's something else you need to know, *fratello*. Santa Palazzo belongs to our father. In Key West he goes by the name Frank *Palazzo*."

The news was such a shock that for a full minute Joey didn't speak. Finally, he asked, "You're absolutely sure? There's no mistake?"

"None. He's owned the estate for twenty-four years."

"And Rhea's been there since she left town?"

"I'd like to say I've confirmed that, but I haven't. But my gut tells me she's been there the entire three years. She looked relaxed. Talked to the guards. Smiled. Laughed. What I'm saying is, she's no prisoner."

"If that's true, then Frank helped her run."

"We both know he was upset when you broke off your engagement to Sophia D'Lano."

"You're saying he paid Rhea off?"

"Maybe. When Frank wants something bad enough, money's no object. Then, neither is using a power play. He could have cut Rhea a deal. He could have told her she could keep the baby if she cooperated with him."

"You think he knew she was pregnant."

"Frank's a cunning son of a bitch. Sure he knew. How, I can't say, but that's what motivated him. That's what my gut tells me."

"She could have gone to Frank. Maybe she blackmailed him."

Lucky raised his heavy brows. "That's an interesting twist. You think she's capable of that?"

Three years ago Joey would have said no. Today all he could think about was that she had denied him his child.

"I'm not saying it didn't happen that way," Lucky stated. "But the Rhea I remember didn't seem capable of blackmail. She never even bad-mouthed her psychotic ex-husband.''

''That's because she was too busy surviving Stud's hell, to spend time thinking of much else,'' Joey reasoned, showing more emotion than he would have liked.

''Rhea doesn't strike me as the manipulative-bitch type. Soft-spoken and kindhearted comes to mind. I can't pinpoint what made her sexy as hell three years ago. I mean, it wasn't exactly due to the condition she was in—the bruises and all—but she had something that made a man look twice. We both can't deny that.''

More than a dozen qualities had made Joey look twice at Rhea Williams. And any one of them could be blamed for why he had ignored his own rules and mixed business with pleasure.

Up to that point he hadn't wasted his time on married women, or divorced women packing baggage. And Rhea had had one helluva lot of baggage. Her ex-husband had been a cop. And if that hadn't been enough to make Joey steer clear of her, the fact that Stud Williams was a dirty cop working for Frank should have.

''Remember when Frank offered to spearhead your investigation to find Rhea? Smart move on his part if he was the one hiding her out. My guess is, he put himself in that position to intercept information and to keep you in the dark.''

Joey said, "We never got any good leads. I always thought that was strange."

Lucky nodded, rested his glass of scotch on his long jeans-clad leg. "I traced his flight itineraries for the past year. It wasn't easy. Frank covers his tracks better than a snake on stilts."

"And?"

"I've confirmed eight visits to Key West this past year."

Joey swore, then leapt to his feet. "Why didn't I suspect he was involved in Rhea's disappearance?"

"Because he's good at what he does," Lucky reasoned. "Hell, for twenty-four years he's been living a double life without either one of us knowing it. That kind of determination makes me a little nervous. I wonder what else he's been hiding."

"If he's as good as you say, then, by now he's on his way here to confront me." Joey pointed to the silver chain tucked inside his brother's shirt. "I left my cross on Rhea's pillow."

The cross that nested in the thatch of black hair on Lucky's chest was identical to the ones Joey and Jackson wore. Lavina had given *her boys* the crosses one night when hell had descended on them, and all three boys had survived because they had stuck together. The decision they had made that night had bound them for life.

Lucky arched a brow. "You leave the cross for revenge's sake, or out of concern for her state of mind once she found Niccolo gone?"

Not willing to analyze his actions, Joey said, "I want her to come to me. Face me. If she cares about the boy, she'll come."

"My men tell me Frank arrived at Santa Palazzo a few hours ago. My guess is, he got a call that Niccolo was taken and he flew out there soon after. You're right. If he knows it was you who took Niccolo, we can expect him back here within twenty-four hours."

Joey paced to the window, rubbing his jaw. He hadn't shaved in three days—or slept, for that matter.

"So what do you want to do about Frank?"

"I have my son. That's what I went there for."

"The only reason?"

Joey turned slowly. "What are you saying?"

"I'm saying Frank's been lying to us for years. Maybe it's time we looked into why that is. Maybe we need to find out what he's hiding at Santa Palazzo besides Rhea Williams."

"I'll go along with that."

"And Rhea? What do you plan to do with her once she shows up?"

Joey wanted it to be all about revenge where Rhea was concerned. It would be easier that way. But when he'd walked into Rhea's bedroom at Santa Palazzo he had been stopped cold, struck by her familiar scent filling his nostrils. Struck by the sight of her hairbrush on the vanity with blond strands of hair caught in the bristles. To his disgust he'd opened her closet just to look at her clothes.

"Do you think she knows that her ex-husband is in jail for murder?"

"That's an interesting question." Joey returned to the sofa. "It's rather recent news. I suppose it would depend whether Frank thought it was news he could use to his advantage or not. Either way, at the moment, Rhea should be more afraid of me than her ex."

"Rhea's been through a lot in her life, *fratello*."

"So I'm supposed to go easy on her because years ago she married the wrong man, and his favorite pastime was beating her up?"

"No. I'm saying Frank has more experience in deceiving people than Rhea."

"The bottom line is, she's been hiding my son from me like some dirty secret. And if it was Frank's idea, and she was forced into it, she's had plenty of time to find a way to get a message to me. But from what you've said, it sounds like she's been living content at Santa Palazzo."

Joey wasn't going to accept any excuses. Whatever Rhea's reason was, it wouldn't be good enough. And the minute he laid eyes on her, this crazy feeling constricting his chest and tightening his jeans would burn itself out. He couldn't possibly still care about her, after what she'd done.

"She looks different."

Joey blinked out of his musing and saw Lucky studying one of the pictures. "She looks different because she's not wearing a gauze bandage over her eye or a split lip.'' He couldn't disguise the anger and disgust that tainted his deep voice. He still hated the fact that he hadn't been able to keep Stud from terrorizing her.

His gaze returned to the picture of Rhea walking on the beach. Besides being bruise free, he'd noticed that she'd cut her hair into a straight, carefree style, and it had been bleached almost white from the Florida sun. Her skin no longer made her look as pale as a ghost, and she wasn't painfully thin. There was a gentle curve to her hips and more definition to her breasts. The only thing he could guarantee looked the same were her beautiful long legs.

Angry that he'd taken the time to dissect the picture, he said, ''Not having bruises or gauze bandages doesn't change the facts.''

''Which are?''

''That she's a liar and a thief!'' Joey swore softly, wishing he hadn't raised his voice. He didn't want his son to wake up to the sound of his father shouting like an angry fool. He didn't want Niccolo ever to be afraid of him. Not in the way he'd been afraid of his own father when he was a boy.

He and Lucky had tiptoed around their father, beginning at an early age, to avoid his lectures on loyalty to the *famiglia,* but they hadn't been able to escape the hourly drills Frank had forced on them to make his sons weaponry experts. By age thirteen Joey could nail a target dead center with a six-inch knife from twenty yards away. Lucky, at age ten, could empty a round of ammo into a dummy's head with a 25-caliber Beretta and a .38 Special.

More softly, but just as angrily, he said, "She kept me from my son, Lucky."

"Yesterday you had a right to be angry, *mio fratello*. But today you have the boy. Focus on what you want tomorrow. What you want next month. Next year. What you want for Niccolo's future."

"What I want for my son is for him to grow up happy, doing whatever the hell it is he wants to do with his life. I don't want him to be like us. I don't want him to feel trapped, or forced into chasing another man's dream."

Lucky raised his glass of scotch. "Then, we'll drink to happiness, and to changing the future for him."

Joey lifted his glass. "And we'll drink to you, Lucky. For making a trip to Florida and buying that camera."

Lucky nodded, his grin softening his dark eyes and the scar on his chin. "To Niccolo. May he grow up to be as wise as his father, and—" he grinned "—as handsome as his uncle."

Chapter 2

The sight of the milky blue horizon over Lake Michigan was glorious, but it had been as fleeting a feeling as the absurd emotional tug that Rhea had somehow come home…home to stay.

Now, as she stood in the lobby of Masado Towers with a lump in her throat, clutching Nicci's teddy bear, she knew the depth of what she was facing.

The night she'd left Chicago, escorted to the airport by two of Frank's bodyguards, Joey's dream had been nothing more than a blueprint, steel girders and concrete columns. Today, Masado Towers was a work of art, an architectural phenomenon. A city within a city.

Not only was the Towers a grand hotel, but there were condominiums, offices, department stores, boutiques, an art museum, a health club, a grocery store, restaurants, lounges, movie theaters and a bank.

Rhea had never thought she'd underestimated Joey's ability. But all of this confirmed that the man she thought she knew was as complex as the dynasty he had built and now commanded.

If she had known before he had touched her what a mega-power he was, or what the future would hold, would she have done things differently? It was a question she couldn't answer. That night three years ago, beaten down and desperate, alone and scared, she hadn't expected to be rescued—least of all, rescued by Joey Masado.

Countless times she'd gotten herself home from the hospital after one of Stud's outbursts. She could have done it one more time. Then Joey had appeared and completely disarmed her with his take-charge tenderness.

But that was then, and this was now. Last night he had breached a secure compound and stolen his son from under the noses of eight armed guards. And he had done it without a single confrontation. The tender man beneath the tough-guy veneer had a ruthless side. Maybe she had always known that. The rumors had surely warned her that the Masado men never turned the other cheek. Never... And she had seen evidence of that with Frank. He was a hard man, determined to protect his family, whatever the cost.

Rhea checked her watch. It was early, barely eight. She hadn't slept, nor could she until she saw her son

and knew he was safe. She eyed the glass elevator—
the woman at the front desk had said, "You'll find
Mr. Masado's personal elevator in the passageway.
Go down hall B, you won't be able to miss it."

As if in a trance, Rhea stepped into the glass box,
not thinking it peculiar that the door was standing
open as if waiting for her. She pushed the only button
visible, and when the door closed, she wet her lips,
then nervously brushed her long bangs closer to the
scar next to her eye.

When the elevator stopped, she buried her free
hand—the one that was shaking—in the pocket of
her brown suede jacket and waited for the door to
open. When it did, she was confronted by a man who
reminded her of the guards at Santa Palazzo—big
and tough, and capable of snapping a woman's neck
in a split second.

"Ms. Williams?"

"How did you know who I... Never mind."

The blond powerhouse surprised Rhea with a
smile. "I'm Gates. Mr. Masado's—"

"Bodyguard," she finished.

"At the Towers we use the word *assistant*. This
way, Ms. Williams."

Rhea followed the six-foot-five *assistant*. As they
walked along, she saw him lower his head and speak
softly into a small gold lapel pin on his suit jacket.
She decided he was outfitted with a miniature microphone of some kind that allowed him to speak to
his boss.

Moments later, Gates stopped in front of a massive pair of doors. He didn't bother to knock, just swung the door open and moved aside to allow her entry.

Rhea stepped inside, her son's teddy bear gripped tightly in her hand. She didn't know what she had expected to find, but a room shrouded in darkness wasn't it. In the next few seconds, as the door clicked behind her, she saw that a vast wall of closed vertical blinds behind a sweeping half-circle desk were responsible for the shadows. They hadn't stolen all the light from the room, but it certainly had set the tone for what undoubtedly was Joey's morning mood.

The expensive leather chair behind the desk was empty. She was in the lion's den, but where was the lion?

She scanned the room and located a silhouette seated at a mile-long bar that looked like it should have been in a nightclub instead of in an office. There was a liquor bottle on the marble surface, and beside it, a half-empty crystal glass.

It was too early to be drinking, but then, her ex-husband had drunk all hours of the day and night. The comparison, as well as the result of those painful times, didn't calm her nerves.

He knew she was here. Rhea saw him stiffen on the bar stool. It was ever so slight, but she'd learned the hard way to be alert. Even the smallest body changes, a shifting eye or a tightening in the jaw, could be a warning.

The key to handling fear was to keep the brain

well supplied with oxygen so your thought processes remained clear and your reaction time was lightning quick. Knowing this, Rhea concentrated on slow, deep breathing.

A minute ticked by, then two.

She stood there motionless while he raised and lowered his drink. When the glass was empty, he set it down and gave it a little shove. The heavy glass slid smoothly to the end of the bar with less than an inch to spare. It was a practiced maneuver, she decided, perfected over time.

Another minute lapsed before the white leather stool slowly rotated. Rhea's heart skipped several beats, then several more when his dark eyes finally locked with hers.

Joey Masado was an awesome looking man. She had always thought so. Over six feet tall, he had brown bedroom eyes, jet black hair and a body that looked like it had been crafted out of iron.

His hair was shorter than she remembered—more businesslike, and a contradiction to the growth of whiskers that lined his jaw. It appeared he hadn't shaved in three or four days. The stubble, however, didn't detract from his handsome face, it simply added another measure of danger to an already dangerous man.

A minute dragged by before he spoke, but when he did, his deep voice sent raw chills racing the length of her spine.

''Rhea, in the flesh. After all this time, in a heartbeat she returns as quickly as she left. What brings you to town, darlin'?''

Rhea fought the constriction in her lungs, the sudden weakness in her knees. ''You know what brought me, Joey.''

''I'm not sure that I do.''

He was going to make her say it. ''Where's Nicci? Where's my son?''

''You mean 'our son,' don't you, Rhea?'' He came off the stool in one fluid motion, gestured to the stuffed animal in her hand. ''Is that the bear he keeps asking for?''

''Yes. He sleeps with it.'' She expected him to be wearing one of his expensive suits. Instead, he wore jeans and a black V-neck sweater that revealed a dusting of black hair on his chest.

Joey was known for his Sicilian charm and lazy smile, but both were absent as he held out his hand for the bear.

Rhea shook her head, pulled the bear close. ''I want to see him. I want to see my son.''

''No.''

''I need to see him, Joey. I need to know that he's all right.''

''He's fine.''

''Prove it.''

''I don't have to prove a damn thing to you, Rhea.''

''Let me give him the bear, and tell him…''

''Tell him what?''

"That I love him. That everything is going to be all right."

"Is it?"

Rhea's chin started to quiver despite her best attempts to remain strong.

Suddenly he swore. The vulgar words were followed by several more in Italian. Finally he shouted, "He's my son, damn you! How dare you steal my flesh and blood?"

"Steal? I didn't steal him, Joey."

His nostrils flared as he regarded her with cold eyes. "When were you going to tell me about him, Rhea? When he was five? Ten? Twenty?"

Rhea refused to give in to the urge to scurry behind his desk. She'd been in similar situations before—a hundred times before. She knew better than to cower, or run. Standing her ground, she said, "He's my son, too. I gave him life."

He gave a rude snort. "That's the controversy of the century, darlin'. I believe *I* gave him life."

His words sent Rhea's eyes down his hard body to that area that…yes, had been responsible for giving her son life. Feeling caught, she jerked her gaze back up. "Tell me when I can see my son?"

"When hell freezes. How does that sound?"

"It sounds like something Stud would say, not you."

Another string of Italian obscenities scolded the air.

"You have so much, Joey. All I have is Nicci. A child needs his mother."

"But not his father?"

"I never said that. Never wanted that."

"What did you want, Rhea?"

She had wanted to share their son. To be a family. But that hadn't been possible. "I wanted my baby born healthy."

Her words gave him pause. "And is he healthy?"

"Yes."

"What kind of mother denies a child his father, Rhea? A father who wants him and has the means to take care of him? If a child can't trust his mother to have his best interests at heart then who the hell can he trust?"

Rhea's own mother had walked out on her when she was seven. A few years later her father had died, and she'd been placed in an orphanage. From the minute Nicci was born, all her energy had centered around being a good mother to him. No, not just a good mother—the best mother ever.

"You can accuse me of many things, but not of being a bad mother. Nicci can trust me, Joey. I've kept him safe and warm and happy since the second I learned I was pregnant."

"The way I see it, what you kept him was father-less."

"That wasn't my fault."

"You're the one who left. He didn't even know about me until last night."

"You told him you're his father?"

"I am his father. Yes, I told him."

Rhea rarely swore, but she did now. "Dammit, Joey, you're a stranger to him. Scaring him half to death in the middle of the night, then confusing him about who he is... You—"

"He's not confused or scared."

"How the hell would you know what he is? You've been a father less than twenty-four hours."

"Not by choice."

Rhea squeezed her eyes shut, her concern for Nicci escalating. She didn't realize she'd forgotten to breathe until a wave of dizziness stole her balance. She swayed, but before she fell, a strong hand gripped her upper arm. Startled, she blinked her eyes open to find Joey directly in front of her. His fingers bit into her arm as he stared down at her. Unable to hold his gaze, she looked past him to their reflection in the large gilded mirror behind the bar.

Joey's size dwarfed her, and again she realized that she was no match for him, and that maybe it would have been smarter to wait for Frank.

Suddenly he let go of her arm and walked around her. "One or two scars... Not bad. You didn't lose your eye."

From the mirror, she watched as he studied her as if she were on an auction block. He circled again, this time stopping behind her. Leaning in, his lips brushed her ear. "Were you able to nurse my son?"

The question might have seemed strange, even crude, to anyone else, but Rhea knew why Joey had asked it. Her dance with death had kept her in chest bandages for weeks. She had still been in them when she'd left town. Nonetheless, the intimacy of the question brought a hot flush to her cheeks. She had slept with this man, had come apart in his arms, yet their affair hadn't really gotten under way until after Stud had put her through her bedroom window and in danger of losing her eye and her right breast.

He came around and faced her. "Well?"

The heat from her cheeks spread over her face and down her neck. She'd agreed to some reconstructive surgery to repair the damage, but then she'd learned she was pregnant and had decided against it. "Yes, I nursed Nicci." Not waiting for him to delve into her answer and embarrass her further, she stated, "Are you telling me you're not going to let me see my son, Joey?"

"He's not here. He's spending the morning with a friend."

Rhea tensed. "He's with a stranger. Can you trust this person?"

"I wouldn't have left him with her, otherwise."

Her. Sophia D'Lano… He'd left their son with his wife. "Is she competent?"

"Of course she's competent."

"How can you be sure? Nicci's a very active child. If you're not used to dealing with children, then—"

"Lavina Ward is used to children. And she would never let anything happen to my son."

That was not the answer Rhea had been expecting.

Not at all. "Are you saying Jackson's mother is watching over Nicci right now?"

"That's right."

Jackson Ward wasn't only Joey's friend, he was her friend, too. At least, he had been three years ago. He had worked with her ex-husband at the police department. He was, however, nothing like Stud. Jackson was good and honest, and his mother was the reason he had grown up that way. She was a hard-working woman who supported her family as the owner of Caponelli's Restaurant in Little Italy.

"She's agreed to help me out until I can hire a nanny."

Rhea's maternal instinct flared. "Nicci doesn't need a nanny, Joey. He needs his mother."

"But not his father?"

"All right, yes, we made a baby. And, yes, I didn't tell you. But you weren't honest with me, either. You never told me you were engaged to Sophia D'Lano." She spun away from him and walked deeper into his spacious office. Turning, she said, "I'm telling you right now, the only way your wife will raise my son is over my dead body, Joey. Do you hear me? I won't abandon him out of fear of what you'll do to me."

"Wife? What the hell are you talking about?"

"Don't bother denying it, Joey. Your father told me about her."

"The engagement, Rhea, was called off. I never married Sophia."

His words hit her like a straight-line wind off the Gulf.

"You left Chicago because Frank told you I was getting married? Is that the story you're selling?"

It was more complicated than that. Far more complicated. Rhea heard herself say, "Our baby's health was the most important thing. If you remember, I had my hands full trying to keep my ex-husband from killing me. Sooner or later, Stud would have shown up again. In bandages and pregnant, what chance did I stand against him?"

"So good old Frank offered you money and a free ride out of town, and you jumped on."

"It wasn't exactly like that."

"How exactly was it?"

"I hadn't been able to work. Money was an issue, but that's not what he offered. What he offered was something better than cash. He offered me a new life without pain, and a promise that Nicci would be safe."

"At Santa Palazzo?"

"Yes. He guaranteed me that our child would be born in a safe environment. And he promised I would be able to raise him. You got Sophia, and…I got our baby. It seemed fair."

Unexpectedly he moved, closing the distance between them so quickly that Rhea thought he was going to strike her. But instead, he curled his arm around her waist and jerked her up against his hard thighs. "Has Frank touched you?" he demanded. "Have you been in my father's bed?"

"No."

"The truth, Rhea!"

The question was absurd. Yes, she was close to Frank. He had become like a father to her.

"I'll have the truth, damn you!"

"Frank hasn't touched me, not in the way you mean. But he has been good to us. When he finds out what you've done, he's not going to like it. He'll come, and—"

"Rescue you again?" He shook his head, laughed bitterly. "No, darlin', not this time. He'll have to go through me first. And trust me, Frank's not that stupid. He'll come, that's a given, but my son won't be going back to Santa Palazzo. And if you want to see him anytime soon, you won't be leaving, either."

Chin high, Rhea promised, "I won't abandon my son, Joey."

"Then you've just limited your options, darlin'."

What did he mean by that? The moment Rhea asked herself the question, he slid his hands down her back and curved them around her small backside. He had money to burn, as the saying goes. If he wanted it, or thought he needed it, he likely already had it. She had nothing of value to offer him. Nothing but...

He pressed himself against her, kept his eyes locked with hers. "Maybe some kind of an agreement can be made that will satisfy both parties."

She knew what he was suggesting, and the idea of sleeping with Joey made Rhea's knees weak. Three years ago the sex between them had been incredible. What would it be like now, bandage-free?

Bandage-free, but not scar-free.

Her voice half strength, shaky, Rhea said, "I'll do anything, Joey. Anything but that. I won't sleep with you."

The idea of having her naked beneath him took Joey's aroused state and pushed him over the edge. Stone hard and angry as hell, he shoved Rhea away from him, then turned his back on her.

He had every right to take his child, dammit. Every right to want to hurt her. He was justified, dammit!

Then, why did he feel so damn guilty?

Because if she was telling him the truth, it changed everything. She was right about Stud Williams. If he had learned she was pregnant, he would have been just that much more determined. And she was right about Sophia, too. He had planned to marry her—in the beginning.

Joey studied Rhea holding onto Niccolo's bear. Her high-necked blue sweater matched her sapphire eyes. Her jacket was short and it sent his gaze down her long legs, then slowly back up. It was impossible to look at her lovely legs without remembering how damn good they had felt wrapped around his waist.

Lucky was right. Three years ago there was an

unexplained beauty about Rhea. But today she wasn't just beautiful, she was sexy as hell. And that, coupled with the fact that she was the mother of his child and the woman he had never been able to forget, was keeping his chest tight, and the constriction inside his jeans at a choke-hold level. He'd hoped that after their meeting he would be able to set her aside and concentrate solely on his son. But the fact remained that he still wanted her. More than ever.

"Where are your bags?" he demanded.

His question must have surprised her, because she floundered for an answer. "Uh...I have a room at the Fairmont."

Joey strolled to his desk and pressed a button on his phone panel. "Gates, get someone over to the Fairmont to pick up her bags. *Capiche?*"

"Right away, Mr. Masado."

From behind his desk, he went back to studying her heart-shaped face. She had always been too pale, but now her skin was a honey brown and the contrast with her white-blond hair was magnificent.

Her right eye had been patched shortly after he'd met her. The doctors had given her less than a fifty-fifty chance of saving it. Now, the only evidence that she'd experienced hell were two white lines that disappeared into the corner of her eye, and a thin scar on her lower lip.

He moved on to her lush mouth, remembering how the slowly healing cut had prevented him from kissing her with any amount of passion. But there was nothing stopping him from kissing her now.

Angry that she still owned a significant part of his body and his mind, that she likely always would, Joey said, "You'll stay here at the Towers. But for now, you won't go near Niccolo."

He heard her suck in her breath, watched her lean over as if she was going to be sick. Her blue eyes were instantly liquid with tears.

"Joey, please. Let me have five minutes with him. Please."

He turned his back on her, walked to the window and pulled open the blinds to let in the morning sun. Minutes passed before he turned to address her once more. "Stud was arrested four days ago. It seems he's not only a wife beater but a murderer."

She gasped. "He murdered someone?"

"Actually, three people. Remember when Tom Mallory was killed just before you left town? Stud was the one who shot him. Several weeks ago, he killed Milo Tandi and a dancer at the Shedd. I won't bore you with the details. I just thought you'd feel better knowing that he's locked up."

"He killed Tom? Why?"

"Because he thought you were sleeping with him. He also tried to kill Jacky and me for the same reason."

"Oh God."

She was shaking. In spite of his attempt to remain indifferent, Joey said, "He's crazy, Rhea. The best place for Stud Williams is six feet under, but instead he's going to Joliet Prison. I guess that's the second best place for him.''

She brushed at a tear clinging to her scarred eye. ''Joey, let me see Nicci. Just for a minute. Let me explain why I won't be seeing him for a while, so he doesn't think I've abandoned him.'' More tears. ''Please.''

Joey stepped forward and pressed another button on his phone panel. The action brought the door swinging open and Gates into his office.

''Yes, Mr. Masado.''

''Find a suite for Ms. Williams. Something with a view. She'll be spending a lot of time staring out the window.''

Chapter 3

As Joey had so cynically implied she would do, Rhea spent much of the day in front of the living room window, watching the clouds go by.

At times she had gotten so restless that she had paced her plush prison on the forty-sixth floor, wringing her hands and asking herself the same question that plagued her since she faced her son's father. If she had agreed to sleep with Joey, would he have given in and allowed her to see Nicci?

Rhea touched her eye. She didn't have a model's looks, but she was no longer wearing an eye patch and sporting bruises. She'd never been comfortable wearing a lot of makeup, but she'd practiced enough so that the scars on her face were nearly invisible. She'd even taken a hairdresser's advice and had her hair cut to hide the scar at her temple.

She wasn't flawless, but... Flawless or not, Rhea admitted, if she got the opportunity to strike a deal with Joey a second time, she would do whatever he asked. If it guaranteed her time with her son, she had no choice.

A knock sounded at the front door sometime after seven. Rhea quickly turned from the window and hurried to answer. Her hand on the doorknob, she peeked out the peephole. When she saw who stood outside, her heart sank.

She hesitated just for a second, and in that second, she saw Joey's younger brother pull a key from his pocket. Lucky was ten times more frightening than Joey, but Rhea refused to be intimidated. If she didn't stand up for Nicci, who would?

She opened the door. "What do you want?"

"You. Upstairs."

Not opening the door any wider than the width of her body, Rhea asked, "Why?"

"Because there's a problem."

"A problem? With Nicci?"

Without answering the question, he knocked the door open and grabbed her arm. "We're wasting time. Move it."

She shook off his hand and bolted for the elevator. In minutes they were on the top floor of the tower, passing Gates—who looked anxious and very glad to see her.

The minute she stepped into Joey's penthouse, Rhea could hear Nicci's screams. Frantic, she hurried through the amber-lit foyer and into the living room, barely noticing its lavishness.

"He's in the bathroom at the end of the hall." Lucky pointed to a hall that disappeared around a dramatic S-shaped wall. "Joey was going to give him a bath before he put him to bed."

"A bath? Oh, no!" Rhea hurried down the hall, led by Nicci's screams. She thrust open the bathroom door, then stopped dead at the sight of Joey standing in the middle of a square red bathtub. He was fully clothed in an expensive white shirt and gray suit pants, his jaw was set, and he was trying to restrain their hysterical, naked son.

"Nicci, stop before you get hurt!"

The seriousness in her tone brought Joey's and Nicci's heads around. Her son immediately stopped thrashing, then thrust out his arms. "Mama! No baff, Mama. No…baff."

Rhea stepped forward, surprised when Joey thrust Nicci at her. She eagerly took him, and Nicci twined his arms around her neck. His little body was trembling, and she cradled him while she searched for a towel to wrap around him.

Facing Joey, she said, "There was an accident on the beach at Santa Palazzo. It happened about a year ago. Nicci was pulled under by the ocean's current. Since then, he's been terrified of water."

"How the hell did that happen? Weren't you watching him? What kind of mother—"

"Don't say it, Joey. I was holding onto his hand. He was only under water for a few seconds."

"But long enough to make him afraid of a damn bathtub for the rest of his life?"

"Don't swear," she said softly, careful not to chastise Joey too strongly in front of his son. "Not unless you want him using that word in school in a few years."

Rhea kissed Nicci's silky black head, then turned and assessed the bathroom. Spying the large sink in the middle of a ten-foot vanity, she pulled the stop, then ran warm water into it.

"Nicci, honey, let go of Mama's neck. That's a good boy." She winked at him as his dark eyes met hers. Then she kissed his nose. "Shall we play?"

When he nodded, she eased him from her and placed him on the vanity. Making sure the towel was beneath him, she checked the temperature of the water, then added a little more warm before sliding his bare feet in. "Doesn't that feel good, Nicci? Wiggle your toes."

He did more than wiggle his toes. He kicked out both feet and sent water up the front of Rhea's blue sweater and down the front of her jeans. The second kick lifted the water to the mirror and onto the white tiled floor.

Instead of reprimanding her son, she said, "Joey, a washcloth, please."

Rhea heard him step out of the tub, heard him swear again, a little more softly this time and in Ital-

ian. From somewhere behind her, a thick white washcloth sailed over her shoulder and plopped into the
water. Then the door closed, and she was left alone
with her son.

A half hour later, Rhea tucked the teddy bear next
to Nicci in his bed and kissed his cheek. "If you
need Mama, just call out. I'll hear you. I promise."

She turned around and found Joey standing in the
doorway. He'd changed into a pair of dry pants—
jeans that showed off his lean hips and long legs. A
steel-gray V-neck sweater covered his broad shoulders and revealed a hint of black hair on his chest.

He'd shaved, but it didn't soften his set jaw. He
was angry with her, possibly even more so now than
he had been that morning.

When he backed up, she walked out and started
down the hall. Trailing her, he said, "Not too smart
making promises you can't keep, Rhea. Tomorrow
Niccolo will have a nanny, and all of his needs will
be met by a professional."

Rhea spun around. "Are you so sure she'll be able
to meet all of his needs, Joey? If she had been here
tonight, she would have attempted to bathe Nicci,
just like you did."

"Your point?"

"My point is that no matter how good your nanny
is, she won't be able to replace me. Nicci's afraid of
water, and you can tell that to your professional, after
you've frightened your son half to death. But do you
know what to tell her about his allergies, or are you

planning on jumping feet-first into *that* unknown territory, too?''

"Allergies? What kind of allergies? You said he was healthy.''

"He is healthy. Just allergic to carrots.''

"Carrots? What else?''

Rhea hesitated, then said, "I should let you find out the hard way, Joey. But at whose expense? It wouldn't be yours or your professional's, it would be at Nicci's expense. Still, a nanny won't know that he likes peas better than squash. Or that thunderstorms make him wake up crying. Or that he gets constipated if he doesn't drink enough juice. But I know those things, Joey. I know them because I've been with our son every minute since he was born.'' On a roll, she jabbed herself in the chest. "Me! The only professional he needs! His mother!''

He reached out and covered her mouth with his hand. "We're not going to fight in the hall where he can hear us,'' he whispered hotly.

Rhea opened her mouth and bit down hard on the side of his hand, so frustrated and angry that she reacted before she thought.

"Maledizione!"

The minute she let go, she warned him off with her extended arm. "I'm the one who should be caring for our son. But have it your way…*daddy*. Father knows best, right?''

She turned then, and quickly headed for the door. She didn't want to go, but he was going to send her back to her cell "with a view," anyway. At least this way, she wouldn't have to be led away like a criminal on her way back to lockup.

She'd almost reached the door when he caught her in the foyer and turned her around. Backing her against the wall, he easily pinned her there. He leaned in and snapped, "Damn you, Rhea... Damn your hide."

"And damn your hide right back, Joey. Now let go! Or I'll—"

"Or you'll what?"

Instead of telling him, Rhea hoisted her knee.

As she clipped him in the crotch, Joey swore, then wedged his knee between her legs and gave her his weight. "You should have told me you were pregnant, damn you."

"You should have told me you were engaged to Sophia D'Lano."

"I'm Niccolo's father."

"I'm his mother."

The room fell silent as he stared her down. A full minute lapsed before he said, "Then, the answer is simple, isn't it?"

His voice was no longer full of anger, but of resignation.

"Nothing is simple when it comes to you, Joey. Not one damn thing."

He raised his hand and brushed a finger over the scar on her lower lip. "Say it? Say you'll do what-

ever you have to, for the sake of our son. I want to
hear you say it.''

If she refused him this time, she might never see
Nicci again. Never hold him, or hear his sweet voice
call her "Mama." Life wouldn't be worth living
without her son, and she was sure Joey had figured
that out. He knew he had her boxed into a corner. A
very tight corner.

Her chin quivered, but Rhea kept it up, anyway.
"Okay, Joey," she whispered. "I get to care for
Nicci, and—"

"I get whatever I want."

There was more silence. Rhea's chin continued to
tremble, and Joey's eyes bored into her as if he was
waiting for her to change her mind. But she wasn't
going to, and when another minute passed, he
dropped his hand and stepped back.

"There's an empty bedroom across the hall from
Niccolo's room. You can move your things in there.
Tomorrow morning, meet me in the sunroom at
seven sharp. I'll tell the cook she has the morning
off. Two eggs, three strips of bacon, juice and coffee,
Rhea. Questions?''

She shook her head.

He turned and swung the door open. "Gates, Ms.
Williams is moving again. Get somebody downstairs
to pack her things."

"And where will she be moving to, sir?"

Rhea heard several graphic words, all of them in
Italian. Then, "Where do you think, Gates?"

"Sir?"

More Italian. "Get her suitcases up here within the hour, Gates. *Capiche?*"

Joey headed for the Stardust Bar on the tenth floor of Masado Towers, intent on getting drunk. The idea behind the Open Twenty-Four Hours sign out front was to give the night owls a place to light—all night long, if need be.

With half-moon shaped booths in midnight-blue leather and a million neon stars scattered on a black ceiling, the atmosphere echoed the eclectic food and drinks, especially the latter, with names like Midnight Sun, Pink Cloud and the famous Moonshot.

As Joey stepped inside, he saw Lucky and Jackson seated at a corner table. Flagging a waitress, he ordered a double scotch, then slid into the booth.

"Who's watching Niccolo?"

Joey scowled at his brother. "You know damn well who's up there with him. Why in the hell did you stick your nose in my business? I was handling things."

"You were handling things, all right." Lucky turned to Jackson. "You should have seen it, Jacky. Joey was in the bathtub with his shoes on, juggling my screaming nephew like he was a slippery eel. *Mio fratello* can make a hundred grand a day pushing buttons on his computer, but when it comes to—"

"Shut up, Lucky."

When Jackson chuckled, Joey nailed his best

friend with an ugly look. "I don't want to hear what you're thinking. Save it until I'm in a better mood."

Jackson schooled his grin. "I wasn't going to say anything, Joe."

"Like hell you weren't."

"Well, maybe I was going to make one small comment. An observation."

"Just one?"

"Yeah, one. I was going to say, I'm glad it's you and not me. Becoming an overnight father, I mean." Jackson glanced at Lucky. "Did you get pictures? Nicci's first bath with Daddy? We could put them on Ma's conversation wall at Caponelli's."

Joey swore, then reached for the glass of scotch before the waitress could set it down. After he'd inhaled it, he said, "Let's get drunk."

"Drunk?" Lucky grinned. "Hell, yes. Let's. It always makes me feel better."

Jackson elbowed Lucky. "Joey doesn't need to get drunk. Neither do you."

"Yes, I do," Joey argued. "I just moved Rhea into the penthouse."

Joey ignored Jackson's shocked look and reached for his drink. When he realized it was empty, he looked at Lucky, who appeared more surprised than Jackson. "Get me another bottle, Lucky. No, get two."

After Lucky gestured toward the waitress and held up two fingers, he said, "Things are never black and white. This morning you wanted revenge. Obviously, after getting a good look at Rhea, you've decided on something a little more uplifting.'' His rugged mouth curved into a wry grin. ''Hell, I can't blame you for that. Those photos didn't do her justice. Must have been a poor job of develop—''

''Shut up, Lucky.'' Joey rubbed the back of his neck, the day's events giving him a helluva headache. ''He's afraid of water,'' he said absently.

''Who's afraid of water?'' Jackson asked.

''Niccolo. That's what started this whole mess tonight. There was some kind of accident at Santa Palazzo.'' Joey shoved a fifty-dollar bill at the waitress when she brought the two bottles of scotch. ''Niccolo was on the beach with Rhea and somehow he was dragged under water.'' He looked over at Jackson. His friend's grin was gone, and so was the mischief in his green eyes. ''You're sure Stud Williams is on his way to prison, right?''

Jackson nodded. ''He confessed yesterday.''

''At least that's one problem solved. I don't need to worry about him with Rhea back in town.''

''Sunni's relieved, too,'' Jackson offered.

Sunni Blais was Jackson's soon-to-be wife. He'd been assigned to protect her a few weeks ago. It had been a scary couple of weeks, but in the midst of the craziness, Stud Williams had been charged with murder and Jackson and Sunni had managed to fall in love.

Lucky said, ''Letting Rhea stay with Niccolo should make her happy.''

"Should I care if Rhea's happy?" Joey didn't mean for the question to be answered. "It's Niccolo's comfort level I'm concerned with. But right now, all he cares about is his teddy bear and his mama. You should have seen him when he laid eyes on Rhea. He just about flew out of my arms to get to her."

"He was just scared, Joe," Jackson reasoned.

"He was scared, all right. And I didn't know what the hell to do or say to calm him down."

"That's not your fault," Lucky argued.

Joey knew his brother and Jackson were trying to make him feel better, but it didn't ease his stinging pride. "I thought I had it all figured out this morning. The nanny was going to start tomorrow, Rhea was in a room three floors down—and then all hell broke loose."

"So maybe you shouldn't have moved her in," Lucky considered. "If you want Niccolo to start relying on you, then—"

"Rhea pointed out that I don't know a damn thing when it comes to Niccolo's needs. And she's right. I don't have a clue."

"He's a kid, Joe, not a high-tech robot," Jackson pointed out. "How complicated can he be?"

Lucky motioned to Jackson. "We can help out."

"So now you two are experts on how much juice my son needs to prevent constipation?"

"What?"

"Never mind." Joey stole a cigarette from Lucky's

pack on the table and lit it. Taking a long drag, he reached for his glass of scotch. "You hear anything from Frank?"

"No. He's still in Florida. They've got hurricane winds beating the coast. My guess is he'll be knocking on your door sometime tomorrow if he can get his plane off the ground."

Jackson let out a low whistle.

Joey thought it was in anticipation of his confrontation with his father, but as he followed his friend's gaze to the bar entrance, he saw whom the whistle was meant for.

"Dammit." Joey eyed Sophia D'Lano in royal-blue glitz, noting that the dress advertised her curves like a lit-up billboard for Viagra. "What else can go wrong tonight?"

The minute he'd spoken the words, she spied him and waved, then started over.

Lucky asked, "How do you want to play this? You plan on telling her you're a daddy, or do we keep Niccolo and Rhea a secret for the time being? The latest rumor is that she's determined to get you to the altar before New Year's."

Joey ground out the cigarette. "We don't tell her a damn thing. Not until I talk to Frank."

"What are you doing here, Joey?" Sophia arrived batting her long lashes and smiling like she'd just had her teeth cleaned. "Your secretary told me you were out of town."

"I was." Joey stood, leaned forward and kissed Sophia's flawless cheek.

She glanced at Lucky and Jackson, then at the empty seat. "It looks like there's room for one more." She tilted her head and batted her eyelashes at Joey. Turning slightly, she made sure her breasts brushed his arm. "I haven't seen you in days. Let's catch up."

Joey stepped aside and allowed Chicago's mafia princess to slide into the booth, then sat down beside her. Since their breakup, Sophia had been inching her way back into his life. But for the past three months, she'd been pushing harder than ever. He admitted that she was beautiful, with rich caramel eyes and sooty black hair that fell past her shoulders, but he'd never envisioned himself marrying her.

"So was it business or pleasure?"

"Excuse me?"

"Your trip?" Sophia licked her lips. "Your secretary didn't say. You're not hiding some big dark secret, are you?"

Jackson choked on his beer, while Lucky almost bit in half the cigarette he was lighting. But Sophia didn't notice. She was too busy situating herself closer to Joey so he could look down the front of her dress.

The waitress came and took Sophia's drink order. Two Moonshots later, she was snuggled close to Joey, purring in his ear. Thirty minutes later, Jackson excused himself, claiming he had to go home and rescue Sunni from Mac—Mac being Jackson's once K-9 partner who was now retired and spent most of his time on the sofa watching *Westminster* and dreaming about a long-legged greyhound with an attitude.

Ten minutes after that, Lucky's exaggerated yawn warned Joey that his brother was next in line to desert him. He'd just as soon not be left alone with Sophia. She would likely invite herself upstairs. She'd done it before.

His son's familiar cry warned Joey that he didn't need to worry about that happening. He jerked his attention to the Stardust's lit-up entrance, and there they were, Rhea and Niccolo.

He watched as Rhea scanned the crowd, while his son continued to demonstrate how healthy his lungs were. When Rhea spied him, she started forward, weaving her slender hips through the crowd.

Disaster was only seconds away, and still he sat there while the noose tightened about his neck, stupidly ogling the swell of Rhea's breasts crammed into another high-necked sweater, this one white and damn near iridescent from the black lights shining down from the ceiling.

She came to a halt beside his table, her gaze going first to Sophia, then to Lucky, then finally to him. Over the top of Niccolo's continued crying, she stated, "Your son wants you. He says you promised him a dragon story."

She waited a moment, and when Joey didn't say

anything, she continued. "I don't know that story. He tells me he doesn't want any of the others I usually tell him. He's informed me that 'The Three Blind Mice'...suck. Yesterday that word wasn't in his vocabulary." She offered Lucky an accusing look, then nailed Joey with one hotter than an open blaze chasing gunpowder. "You shouldn't make promises you can't keep...*Daddy*. Or can you?"

Sophia had come out of her Moonshot fog the minute Rhea had used the word *daddy*. She shoved herself upright and squared her shoulders. Joey watched her out of the corner of his eye as she sized up Rhea, then Niccolo. A second later, he heard her gasp. Recognition had obviously dawned, colliding with Sophia's perfect picture of her future as Mrs. Joey Masado.

Suddenly his son stopped crying. After rubbing his sleepy eyes with his tiny fist, he demanded, "Daddy tell daa-gon story." Then, so there was no mistake who he was talking to, Niccolo thrust himself forward and reached out his arms to his father.

Rhea stood next to Joey in the glass elevator and tried not to think about what she'd walked in on at the Stardust. She had actually felt sick when she'd seen Sophia D'Lano almost sitting in Joey's lap.

Her gaze drifted to Nicci in his father's arms. He was so sleepy, and yet he was fighting to stay awake, determined to hear Joey's dragon story. She only hoped Joey knew the story, because Nicci wasn't going to settle for "The Three Blind Mice." It *sucked.*

When the elevator stopped and the door opened, Joey said, "Did you get moved in?"

"Yes." As Rhea stepped out of the elevator, she said to Joey's assistant, "Norman, did you find somèone to see to my list?"

The muscle machine smiled. "I saw to it personally, Rhea. Uh…Ms. Williams. There's a grocery store on level six. I was able to get everything you needed and it was delivered a few minutes ago."

"Norman?"

Joey was scowling at her. Rhea shoved her long bangs out of her eyes. "Yes. Norman. Don't you know your assistant's name?"

"Of course I know his name." Joey's scowl deepened as he nailed Norman Gates, then shifted the same hard look back to Rhea. "What's this list you're talking about? What the hell could you possibly need that I don't have?"

"Don't swear, Joey. Not unless you want—"

"Niccolo swearing at his teachers. Yeah, I got it. So what am I out of, besides a case of prune juice?"

Joey followed Rhea into the penthouse. When the door closed behind them, she said, "Apple juice and orange juice, not prune. And milk. Nicci hasn't acquired a taste for coffee yet, or scotch. And he doesn't have enough teeth to chew steak. Squid is a bit rich, and I haven't introduced him to eggplant or broccoli just yet. And cabbage can be gassy."

She could see that she had completely lost him. Good.

"So I need to keep mushy peas and dog food on hand. Is that what you're telling me?"

"Peas, yes. Dog food only if you plan on buying him a puppy. We also needed protective covers for the outlets and a dozen night-lights. Nicci gets out of bed in the middle of the night. He sometimes comes looking for me. No doubt, he'll come looking for you, too. That's if you can deliver on the dragon story. The protective covers are for the electrical outlets. Children are attracted to them. You'd feel terrible if Nicci stuck his finger in a wall socket."

"No, *he'd* feel terrible. But the good news is, he'll only do it once."

"Not necessarily." Rhea eyed her son, half asleep on his father's shoulder. Nicci had bonded with Joey in an alarmingly quick fashion. For two and a half years he had looked to her for his every need and comfort. But in a matter of one day he'd become captivated by his father.

Angry that Joey seemed to have that effect on both of them, she said, "Are you going to tell him that dragon story you promised or was that just a lie?"

"I know a dragon story."

Rhea snapped her mouth shut. She had a hard time envisioning Frank Masado sitting on the edge of his son's bed telling him a fairy tale. She could, however, picture him demonstrating how to beat the hell out of someone. Survival 101 before age ten was no doubt required in the *Mafia Handbook*.

She watched as Joey headed down the hall to Nicci's bedroom. She had the urge to follow, just to make sure that the story actually existed. She resisted—that is, until fifteen minutes had passed and her curiosity got the better of her.

Outside the bedroom, she stood quietly and peered inside. She'd expected to see Nicci in bed, but the bed was empty. She scanned the room and found Joey sitting in a rocking chair that had been pulled close to the window. He was rocking slowly. The dragon story must have been told to Nicci's satisfaction, because he was now snuggled against Joey's chest with his eyes closed.

The sight brought tears to Rhea's eyes. That first year she had held onto the hope that things would change, that Joey would come looking for her at Santa Palazzo. Night after night, she had walked the beach, hoping he would suddenly appear. She'd been dedicated to the dream, but that's all it had ever been—a silly dream.

In your dreams, baby girl. That's the best place to live. Poor folk like us live in our dreams.

The memory of her mother's desperate words followed Rhea into her bedroom across the hall. Exhausted, but too restless to sleep, Rhea prowled the elegant room decorated in shades of blue and silver.

Like the rest of the penthouse, the furniture was lush and the windows oversize. Nowhere in the entire penthouse could you escape feeling surrounded by Chicago's amazing skyline.

The bed was of gray iron, the headboard high and ornate, with corner posts at least ten feet tall. The blue comforter that went to the floor had silver threads woven through it, the pillow shams more silver than blue. The carpet was the color of ash and at least an inch thick. After an hour of pacing, Rhea opted for a shower to help her relax. Afterward, feeling marginally better, she left the private bathroom, tying the belt of her black satin robe.

She didn't realize she wasn't alone until she had come fully into the room. Stopping abruptly, she saw Joey standing near the window, looking outside. Without provocation, he turned, his eyes moving over her slowly from head to toe.

Rhea's heart began to pound the second he started toward her. Again her body was anticipating his touch the way it had years ago—the way it had that morning.

He stopped mere inches from her and reached for the ties on her robe. Instinctively, Rhea grabbed his hand. "Joey, please. Can't we talk about this. I mean, I—"

"The deal was, you get to care for Niccolo and I get whatever I want. What I want tonight is you in my bed."

Rhea knew what she'd agreed to. And under different circumstances, she would have surrendered to him. Only, she wasn't the same person any longer.

She had been left scarred, and she was sure he didn't realize just how bad it was.

For a time she'd just felt ashamed, but now she felt protective of her body, and she'd vowed never to let anyone hurt her again.

She said firmly, "I can't do this, Joey. I thought I could, but you don't understand."

"I understand that we made a deal."

"I know that, but—"

"Do you have someone in Florida you care about?"

"No. It's not that. I just can't let you touch me."

She could feel heat creeping up her neck and into her cheeks, feel her throat closing off and her eyes stinging. She tried to move past him, but he threaded his fingers through the belt and yanked her up against him. Thinking he meant to force her, Rhea panicked and slapped him.

He released her suddenly, and for a moment he just stood there, then stalked to the open door. There he stopped and turned back. "What is in my home, I own. You, Rhea, have chosen to be in my home. Therefore, you are mine."

"No! I'm not any man's property. Never again. I'm—"

"Mine… If you don't like that arrangement, darlin', then leave my home tonight. Stay, and I'll assume you're willing to honor our arrangement."

"I'm not leaving my son," Rhea insisted.

"Then, in the future when I ask you a question,

you will give me the truth as you know it. And when I tell you to do something, you will do it no matter what. Don't tell me 'no' again, Rhea." He started into the hall, then turned back. "Tomorrow morning set the breakfast table for two. You'll be joining me."

Chapter 4

The concoction smelled like liquefied waste. Vito Tandi lifted the cup, plugged his nose and drank the smelly swill. A knock at the door had him setting down the stone cup and looking at the diamond-studded gold clock on his desk. Clearing the cobwebs from his throat, he said, "Come in, Summ."

Vito's housekeeper entered his study. She was a small Japanese woman who claimed to be fifty but looked no older than thirty. Her head slightly bowed, she said, "Mr. Trafano is here, *Shujin*. Should I send him in?"

Vito eyed the small woman who had survived his sour disposition for twenty years. "Is he alone?"

"Yes."

"I guess you can't tell him I'm not here. Everyone

in the *famiglia* knows I haven't left Dante Armanno in years.'' Vito's annoyance rose above the sound of the electric heater that hummed near his feet. He hadn't been able to keep his damn feet warm for over a month. His circulation had gone to hell along with everything else in his life.

He had money up the ass, but he still couldn't buy a cure for the cancer that ravaged his throat. Nor could he prevent Moody Trafano from becoming his successor, as long as Carlo Talupa's word was still law in Chicago.

For the past two years Carlo had been preaching about the new-generation *Cosa Nostra*—the young bloods that were going to take over Chicago, and how the old war dog's days were numbered.

Vito thought Carlo had been sipping too much Charbono. There was nothing wrong with the old ways or how they had done business in the past. He might not be able to move as fast as he once had, but his brain still worked.

The problem in Chicago, plain and simple, was Carlo. He had decided it was all about him and no one else. He'd become greedy, wanting what didn't belong to him. He'd become obsessed with his power. The capos and soldiers fronting him couldn't take a piss without his say-so.

Moody Trafano might be one of the new generation young bloods, but Vito could guarantee the moron didn't know the first thing about keeping the boys on the docks happy, or about offering protection to Coop's Diner or any of the other independents down on the docks who were being harassed by Paolo Rizelli's boys on the South Side.

Tandi wasn't just a widely diversified corporation. Vito was one of the few men in the *famiglia* who had continued to take care of his neighbors like in the old days. Yes, he was into big business, but the men who had helped him get there—the sweat-and-blood boys who still worked twelve-hour days—were his street brothers.

Milo… Damn him for getting himself killed, Vito thought. Grace had only given him one son, and now that son was gone. Shot and killed by that no-good Stud Williams, for no sane reason at all.

It was true that he needed a successor, but not Moody Trafano. His corporation needed a man who had both brains and muscle. A man who could prevent mutiny before it was a spark of disgruntled gossip in a back alley. A man respected by his peers, and who would demand allegiance, then lead his men out the door two steps ahead of them.

Could Moody do that? Vito sized up the man as he came through the door. Curling his lips, he thought, *Not if Moody had twenty years' experience on the street and an angel riding on each shoulder willing to carry him.*

He lowered his head and scribbled the last sentence on the letter he'd been writing to his lawyer, then slid it into an envelope and sealed it quickly. When he met the younger man's eyes, he said,

"Henry Kendler is expecting you. Give him this."
He shoved the letter toward Moody. "Then introduce
yourself. Henry's been my lawyer for thirty years.
He'll be your advisor when I'm gone."

Without the slightest hesitation, the young blood's
long fingers snatched up the letter. "This is it. This
is the letter that will make me?"

Vito snorted in disgust, then assessed Moody's
watery blue eyes and unnatural blond hair. "It makes
you nothing, boy. What it gives you is one chance
to be more than Vinnie D'Lano's bastard. If you can
read, you'll have no problem following the instruc-
tions I've left behind in my will. Forget who made
this company and you'll wish you'd been born a
speck of jungle lice living on a monkey's ass."

Neither Vito's gruffness nor his words seemed to
faze Moody. Still grinning like an idiot, he slipped
the letter into the pocket of his long brown coat, then
said, "You plan on coming after me from the grave,
old man?"

"I won't have to, moron. I got friends in low
places who daily take a meat cleaver to the rat-faced
hustlers in this city who piss me off. They've already
been paid to keep an eye on you."

"I'm Carlo's choice."

"You're not mine. And that, moron, puts you on
my butcher's list."

The comment took Moody's grin, but not his ar-
rogance. "How soon do I take over?"

"When I'm damn good and ready to die. I got at

least a month, so don't expect to get cozy in front of my fireplace sipping eggnog for Christmas.''

"Let's hope you go sooner than that. This house is beginning to stink like rotting flesh.''

Vito had the urge to pull out the .38 bolted into a sleeve underneath his desk and send Moody Trafano's brains out his tiny ear holes.

"Carlo told me I should acquaint myself with Dante Armanno. After I see Kendler, I'll be back to nose around the estate. The woman who answered the door, I assume she comes with the place? I hear Asian women are—''

"Touch Summ, and I'll personally eat those freaky eyes of yours out of your brainless head.'' Once again, Vito's fingers itched to reach for the .38.

"You don't scare me. Carlo told me you talk tough, but that you can't even walk without training wheels.'' He gestured to the metal walker that stood at the end of Vito's desk. "You're just taking up space in a world that's already passed you by, old man.''

"Get out, and don't come back until I'm dead and in the ground.''

The young blood left, but he left laughing. When the door closed, Vito sank back in his leather wing chair and closed his eyes. He could feel perspiration on his bald head, and his hands were shaking. He threaded his sausage-shaped fingers together and rested them on his protruding gut. Several minutes passed before he felt enough in control to reach for the velvet cord at the edge of his desk.

The door opened seconds later and Summ entered. "Yes, *Shujin.*"

"The house is cold, Summ. I pay the heating bill, not you. Turn up the damn heat."

"Too much heat not good for you."

"I'm freezing more than my ass off in here, Summ. That's not good for me, either. Even Chansu is frozen stiff." He stabbed his fat finger in the direction of the blue parrot that sat on the perch in the corner of the room. "He hasn't said a word in the past hour."

"Chansu, meditating. Bring *Shujin* hot tea."

"Not before you turn up the damn heat. And if I can see that white slime floating in my tea this time, you'll be—"

"Matcha make you strong like bull."

Summ bowed her head more deeply, but not before Vito caught the smile that tugged at her thin lips. The damn woman didn't weigh ninety pounds, and still she wasn't afraid of him. Hell, no one was afraid of him anymore. Like Trafano had said, he was just taking up space in a world that had already passed him by. Just a fat old man who stunk like death.

Once Summ backed out the door, Vito glanced at Chansu. He still didn't believe the parrot was Summ's ancient ancestor, but if it made her feel better to think so, then he was willing to play along.

His gaze traveled from the parrot to the picture

hanging on the wall. His wife's life had been short, the end painful for both of them.

"Grace," Vito muttered, "if you had kept your beautiful ass in my bed instead of climbing into Frank's, you would be richer than God right now. More important, you wouldn't have ended up fish bait at the bottom of Lake Michigan, and I wouldn't be handing Dante Armanno over to a moron."

Joey entered the breakfast room the next morning, feeling the effects of too much scotch and not enough sleep. He found Rhea in jeans and a navy-blue sweater, pouring coffee into a cup at the table. His two eggs and three strips of bacon were on the table, along with toast and juice.

He realized that he'd handled things badly the night before. This morning he intended to take things a little slower. At least that had been the plan until he noticed that the table was only set for one. Before he could gentle his words, they were out.

"Dammit, Rhea, I thought I told you to join me this morning!"

"I can't join you when I'm serving you."

Joey stiffened. "If you're trying to see how far you can push me, darlin', I'd advise against it. My home, my rules. Remember?"

"I don't eat breakfast."

"Start. Tomorrow this table will be set for two, and you will have something on your plate. A bagel.

A muffin. Fruit. Fingernails. I don't give a damn what. Something. *Capiche?*''

He tossed his suit coat toward an empty chair and sat. After slapping the white cloth napkin he found next to his plate onto his knee, he reached for the glass of juice. A healthy swig later, he glanced up to find her still standing there, like a maid waiting to serve him.

Scowling, he said, "Sit down, dammit."

She rounded the small table, gathered his jacket and hung it on the back of a vacant chair, then sat across from him.

He picked up the toast, dipped it into his eggs and started to eat. Two bites into his breakfast, he realized she had remembered that he liked one-minute eggs, his toast light and his bacon crisp.

How the hell had she remembered that? They'd eaten breakfast together maybe twice, and if his memory served him correctly, he'd done the cooking both times.

While he chewed, he studied her face. She looked like she hadn't slept any better than he had. "Were you up with Niccolo last night?"

"No. He slept through the night. He's still sleeping."

"Is that normal?"

"Sometimes he sleeps until nine, but not usually. I checked him. He's fine."

Joey dug into his breakfast, enjoying the taste more than he had in ages. His cook couldn't seem to get the bacon any way but limp, and his eggs were always too hard. "Today I want you to make a list of what you and Niccolo will need to be comfortable here. What Gates can't take care of, get Jean to see to. I'll tell her to expect your call. Get the number from Gates." He eyed her high-collared sweater. "You'll need to be specific about your tastes so Jean can get exactly what you need."

"Who's Jean?"

"My secretary."

"Your secretary does your shopping?"

"That's right."

"Well, she's not going to do mine. I'll manage with what I brought until either we're back in Florida or I'm no longer under house arrest."

"Niccolo is staying here, Rhea. He's not going back to Santa Palazzo. The sooner you realize that, the better off you're going to be." When she didn't say anything, he continued. "You're going to need a winter coat. Niccolo, too. Hats. Gloves. Boots. If you remember, Chicago winters can be colder than a witch's ti—" His gaze zeroed in on her chest, then he lowered his head and took another bite of eggs.

"Have you heard from your father?"

"No. But I expect him today. Unless that hurricane decided to move inland."

"He'll come. And when he does, you'll agree to send us back. Frank will insist on it."

She was definitely trying to piss him off.

"He won't let you hurt either one of us."

"Are you trying to pick a fight with me this morning?"

"That would be stupid, Joey. Everyone in this city knows the Masado boys are bullies. What chance do I have against a man who's never lost a fight? That's why Frank—"

He reached out and shoved the last bite of his toast into her mouth. "*Basta!* Enough about Frank!"

As she chewed his toast, he took a sip of his coffee, then rested his arms on either side of his plate. "If you lose a fight in this town, darlin', there's a good chance you won't be breathing the next day. I'm not a bully, I just don't roll over easy."

"Is that what you intend to teach Nicci when he's older?"

He wasn't ready for that question, but in his heart he knew the answer. He would teach his son every clean trick he knew, and all of Lucky's dirty ones twice. Then he'd have him spend some serious time with Jackson. Niccolo would not lack for knowledge, not on any level.

Aware she was waiting for his answer, he leaned forward and locked eyes with her. "I can't change who I am, Rhea. And you can't change the fact that Niccolo is my son. What I intend to do is give him the tools he'll need to become what he must."

"And what must he become, Joey?"

"A survivor, Rhea. I think you'll agree that the most basic skill a person needs to learn is how to survive. When you're backed into a corner, you don't think about what's for dinner, or what you look like, or what other people are saying about you. What you're concerned with is your next breath, and taking it. Nothing else has meaning if you're not sucking air. Am I right?''

She turned her head to stare out the window. "Yes. Of course, you're right. Survival is everything."

He'd intentionally reminded her of what she'd lived through when she had been married to Stud. He hadn't done it to be cruel or insensitive. He'd tossed up the past because he never wanted her to become someone's victim again.

As she continued to stare at the sunrise over the lake, Joey studied her. He'd never seen her without a bruise until yesterday, and that fact hadn't allowed him a moment's peace. Truthfully, now he couldn't get his fill of looking at her.

"Joey, stop."

She turned back to face him, resting her hand next to her eye to hide the scar that was more visible today than it had been yesterday.

"You don't need to do that, Rhea. Hide the scars."

"You keep staring."

"I'm used to seeing bruises. Gauze bandages."

"Bruises…scars. It's really all the same, isn't it?"

"I don't think so. I'm inclined to agree with Lucky. He says a person without scars hasn't lived." Joey reached out and pulled her hand away, then ran his thumb along the two white lines next to her stormy-blue eye. "He says they trace the past and that instead of running from the memory, you should embrace it. He claims it makes you stronger."

"He certainly looks…strong."

Joey caught himself smiling, sensing that wasn't the word she would have liked to use. "Don't let Lucky fool you. He's not as ornery as he looks."

Her hand slid back to the scar next to her eye. "If you say so."

He sobered. "The scars haven't stolen your beauty, Rhea. If you think so, you're not looking in the right mirror."

She made a big deal of glancing at her watch. Obviously uncomfortable with his compliment, she was anxious to make her escape. "If you're usually in your office by eight, you're going to be late."

Joey shrugged, then glanced at his untouched cup of coffee. Cold by now, he suspected. "Could you pour me another cup of coffee and bring it to me? I'll be in my bedroom."

Rhea stood at Joey's bedroom door with his suit coat draped across her arm and a fresh cup of coffee. She took a deep breath, then pushed open the half-closed door.

She had expected his bedroom to be as grand as the rest of his home, but the round bed was definitely a surprise, as was the platform, four steps above the rest of the room, where the bed overlooked the city.

"Rhea, over here."

Rhea blinked, scanned the room and found Joey standing in front of a long glossy black vanity. He was watching her as he straightened his tie in front of a mirror that climbed the wall and reached for the high ceiling.

She stepped into the room, felt the lushness of the white carpet. Walking past a bloodred fainting couch that looked as if it was from another time and place, she neared the vanity where a crystal bowl sat filled with water, floating three lit black candles. The candles, she decided, were responsible for the marvelous exotic scent that filled the room.

She set down the coffee, then stepped back, her gaze traveling to the steps that led to the round bed covered in black velvet with red satin pillows. The large windows behind it were covered with sheer white drapes. Drapes, that, open or closed, didn't conceal the city's skyline.

It looked like the view was the room's art focus— a life-size picture that would be forever changing, depending on weather and time of day.

Self-conscious of how much time she'd spent examining the second level, Rhea headed for the fainting couch and draped the suit coat over the back, then started for the door.

"I'd like you to arrange for the nanny to come by so you can meet her."

His words stopped Rhea. Turning, she said, "I thought we agreed I would care for Nicci."

"We did agree. But once you're no longer under house arrest, as you put it, you'll feel better about leaving him with someone you can trust, right? You can't be with him every second of the day."

"That's where you're wrong, Joey. I've been with Nicci every day since he was born."

"I don't have an ulterior motive here, Rhea. I couldn't run Masado Towers without help—that doesn't make it any less mine. Opal Carvino will be your helpmate, not your replacement. That is, not unless you fly back to Florida."

The last was said to bait her, Rhea decided.

"Opal Carvino's number is in the address book." He motioned to a black leather-bound book on the table next to the couch. "If and when you want to meet her, give her a call. If not today, then maybe tomorrow."

She wasn't going to call the Carvino woman, but she nodded just the same. "I didn't bring cream or sugar. You still take it black, don't you?"

"Black coffee, one-minute eggs and crisp bacon. You got it. Good memory."

He had no idea what all she remembered. Rhea started for the door again. Three steps from escaping him, he called out to her once more.

"Rhea?"

She stopped but didn't turn this time. "What is it, Joey? I should check on Nicci."

"I just did. He's still sleeping. Turn around and face me when I'm talking to you, would you?"

She did as he asked, and found he was no longer watching her in the mirror. He'd turned around, too.

"You'll like Opal Carvino. Trust me on this, Rhea. She has a lot of experience."

She wasn't going to be in Chicago long enough to need Opal Carvino, or to start trusting him. "Just because you're Nicci's father and you have me in a tight spot at the moment, Joey, doesn't mean I'm going to do everything you tell me to do. Not where Nicci is concerned. He's an innocent child who didn't ask to be—"

"Born a Masado." His dark brows furrowed. "You don't need to keep reminding me what kind of legacy I've handed to my son, Rhea."

The heavy regret in his eyes and in his voice gave Rhea pause. She found herself wanting to ease that regret. She shouldn't…shouldn't make herself any more vulnerable than she already was. But there was true sadness in his expression, and so she said what she was feeling—what she had felt from the moment she had learned she was pregnant.

"I'm not sorry Nicci's your son, Joey. You're reading me wrong if that's what you think. He's perfect in every way. My only regret is that—" Rhea stopped, weighed her confession, weighed what it would cost her if she went further.

"Your only regret is what, Rhea?"

"That, instead of Frank, it had been you driving me to the hospital. That it had been you Nicci had walked to when he took his first steps."

It was obvious that wasn't what he had expected her to say. His expression opened up, and in that second Rhea saw that her regret was his own.

Slowly, he came toward her. Rhea wished he would stay where he was, wished she hadn't confessed her true feelings. She needed to be able to think clearly, and she had found out yesterday that when he got too close, she had a hard time focusing on anything but the memories of how it felt to be wrapped in his strong arms.

He kept coming until they were toe to toe, and his masculine scent surrounded her. He said softly, "I wish I had been there, too. You said Frank was there?"

"Yes."

"It should have been me."

The strength and depth of his words made Rhea shiver. Softly she said, "Yes, it should have been you."

"Rhea…"

His gaze had softened, and suddenly he was looking at her with a kind of curious expression. As if he had a dozen questions to ask her. Before he got started, she said, "I'd like to go now."

"Why? Don't you like my bedroom?"

His question sent her gaze back to the bed. "It's a beautiful…room."

Without warning, he wrapped one arm around her and pulled her into the heat of his body. She closed her eyes as he brushed back the hair from her temple.

She could feel his eyes studying the scar he'd uncovered. Seconds later, he lowered his head and kissed the marred flesh, then whispered, ''You've done a good job with our son, Rhea.''

He had no idea what it meant to hear him say that. It was as pleasurable to hear the compliment as to feel his warm lips against her temple. Eyes closed, she relaxed into him, unable to resist.

''Children are so vulnerable,'' she whispered. ''So innocent, and they have so many needs.''

''Everyone has needs,'' he murmured. ''Who's been meeting yours for the past three years, Rhea?''

His words startled her. She blinked open her eyes. ''What?''

''You heard me.''

She looked up, confronted by his intense dark eyes.

''Answer the question, darlin'. Who's been meeting your needs?''

His tone had changed. It was no longer languorous and easygoing. Once again, he was being very direct and…territorial.

She tried to step back, but his arm tightened around her.

''How long, Rhea? How long has it been since you've been kissed? Last week? Yesterday? And touched? When were you last touched…here?'' His hand slid to her backside, and from there, his long fingers made their way vertically along the seam of

her jeans. Curving her backside, he slid them between her legs.

Rhea stifled a moan. "Joey, please..."

Next to her ear, he asked, "If my father kept his
hands off you like you say he did, then who's been
keeping you satisfied, night after night? A guard?
The gardener? Did you entertain a lover on the beach
after midnight? More than one?"

Rhea could feel his heart beating next to her ear,
feel his lower body come alive. Her breasts began to
tingle, and her nipples puckered. Afraid he would
notice, she said, "Joey, stop...please."

He didn't back off. Instead, he gripped her chin so
she could no longer avoid his eyes. His fingers were
still torturing her from behind, still seeking, still
moving and making it difficult for her to breathe.

"I remember, Rhea. I remember how it was. Even
a wounded butterfly has needs."

Rhea felt her cheeks grow hot. "I'm not wounded
any longer, Joey, or needy. Not in the way you
mean."

"So you don't need to feel like a woman anymore?"

He had remembered her words. Those crazy
breathless words she'd spoken to him the first night
he had made love to her. She shook her head. "No."

"Do you expect me to believe you haven't been
touched in three years?"

"I don't care what you believe. I haven't been
kissed or with anyone since you—"

The words had slipped out before Rhea realized what kind of ammunition she had handed him. She squeezed her eyes shut, knowing she'd revealed too much.

"Say that again."

Without looking at his face, she knew he was trying to decide whether to believe her. She'd obviously shocked him. She'd shocked herself. She had never intended to confess such a thing.

She forced her eyes open and tried to pull away from him. When that didn't work, she tried to dodge his eyes, but he easily countered that by moving his free hand to the back of her head to force her to look at him.

His voice was softer when he finally asked, "There's been no one since me? Is that what you're saying, Rhea? No kissing? No touching? No sex?"

She tried to wiggle free, but his hand splayed over her backside and cemented her to him more firmly than before.

He stared at her wet lips. "Three years is a long time, darlin'."

He didn't need to tell *her* how long it had been, and that's why he had to let go of her. As if he read her mind, he gyrated his hips, clearly letting her feel his aroused state.

Oh God…

"You remember, don't you, Rhea? If you remember how I like my eggs and coffee, you sure as hell remember the rest."

"No!" She shook her head wildly. "No, I don't."

"Liar. Open your mouth, darlin'."

"Joey, no!"

"Let's see if you taste as sweet as I remember."

"No!"

"You always liked my tongue. Let's see if you still do."

Slowly he lowered his head, stealing her breath the minute his lips touched hers. Then, like a hot poker, his tongue pushed its way into her mouth.

Seconds later, as Rhea had expected, the kiss turned into a blazing dance of old memories and re-awakened passion. A dance that confirmed she liked his tongue…and remembered everything.

Chapter 5

Her lips were painted bloodred and the color made them look too big. Joey watched Sophia D'Lano glide into his office, wearing half her fortune on her ears and the other half around her neck.

His gaze traveled back to her lips and, without intending to, he began comparing them to Rhea's sexy small mouth. From there, Sophia faded into the woodwork.

It had been the moan that convinced him Rhea was telling the truth. He'd never forget the ache in it, or the way she'd damn near shattered when his tongue entered her mouth. Her response had put the candles on the cake in one damn big hurry, and he'd been ready to carry her to his bed and make love to her all morning long—if Niccolo hadn't appeared in the doorway rubbing his eyes and declaring he was hungry.

"Joey."

His name on Sophia's too-wide red lips brought Joey to his feet. "I'm glad you could make it." He motioned to one of the chairs in front of his desk.

"You've been a naughty boy, Joey. I should be furious with you, but what would be the point?" She brought her white-gloved hands up, shaming him as if he were a five-year-old, then slipped onto one of the leather chairs.

Once she was settled, he sat.

"Men...animals on two legs, my mother used to say. Find one monogamous creature among them and you have to wonder what's wrong with him." She pulled off her gloves, one finger at a time. "The important thing is not to let the situation ruin our future."

Joey set his jaw.

She smiled, read his mind. "Did you think I would throw everything away over one little tramp? It's obvious all she wants is money, Joey. Women can be such manipulative bitches. If last night's little performance wasn't planned, I'll eat my six-carat emerald earrings. So how much does she want?"

Joey sat back and studied Sophia. Vincent D'Lano should be proud. Sophia had turned out as greedy and ruthless as he was.

He said, "When a man sleeps with a woman, he knows what can happen."

"That's what I love about you, Joey. You're a man who doesn't dodge his responsibilities."

Joey knew what she was saying, knew that look. Sophia was suggesting that first and foremost, he had a responsibility toward her. But she was wrong. He had never promised her anything.

"So you're suggesting a settlement and a plane ticket."

"Perfect. You and I really do think alike, Joey."

"But we don't, Sophia. Not at all. I have a son. I didn't plan him, but I want him. He's mine, and I intend to raise him here in Chicago."

"Don't be a fool, Joey. That's what boarding schools are for."

"I like him."

"You like who?"

"My son."

Sophia rolled her eyes. "Oh, please… You're joking, of course. How can you like something that makes that much noise?"

Joey grinned. "He's two and a half, Sophia. Making noise is how he communicates when he's not happy."

"Then, if I scream and cry, will I get my way, too?"

"No."

"What are you telling me, Joey?"

"That you should start shopping somewhere else for a husband."

Sophia's eyes narrowed. "This isn't just about your son, is it. You haven't had your fill of his mother yet, have you."

Silence.

"I've done my homework, Joey. Her name is Rhea Williams and she's so far beneath you it isn't even funny. Her own mother didn't want her, and her father went crazy, then killed himself."

Sophia wasn't telling him anything he didn't already know. After Rhea had disappeared, he had dug up everything he could find on her in hopes that it would help him locate her. He had an entire file on the mother of his child. He knew where Rhea was born, how much she weighed at birth, and what had happened to her after her mother abandoned her. He also knew her father had become an alcoholic shortly after that, and a few years later had stepped off the curb into the path of a city bus.

"There are men who enjoy rutting with low-stationed women—women who will forever be beneath them. They do, however, lack a certain amount of brains and social skills, Joey. You need an asset at your side, not an underfed orphan with sad eyes and bad manners."

Joey glanced around his lavish office. "As you can see, Sophia, I'm not looking for more assets."

"She's that good, is she? You know I can be whatever you want. I'm sure I can be disgusting in bed if that's what you like. All you have to do is tell me what you want."

What he wanted was Sophia gone and out of his life. For good this time. His gaze swept her full breasts—breasts he knew for a fact were flawless and as plump and ripe as melons. But they held no appeal. All he could think about…picture in his mind…was Rhea holding his son as he nursed at her delicate breasts.

Suddenly he stood. "I've got to get to a meeting. I'm glad we could clear this up so quickly."

"But we haven't cleared anything up, Joey. Aren't you forgetting about the deal?"

"What deal is that, Sophia?"

"The one your father made with Carlo Talupa years ago. The one that involved my father."

"I have no idea what you're taking about."

"Of course you… Oh my, you really don't know, do you? Is that why…" She covered her mouth and started to laugh. "Your father never told you."

"Told me what?"

She stood. "Poor Joey."

"Sophia, spit it out."

She shook her head, suddenly smug. "No. I don't think I will. Ask your father, Joey."

"I'm asking you, Sophia."

She continued to laugh, then started for the door. "We'll never be over, sweetheart. Never. My advice is to get that skinny tramp and that noisy brat of yours gone, before it's too late.'' She turned and this time the laughter was gone. ''Then again, don't bother. It's already too late for them.''

''How is Grace doing?''

''She's better. The doctor tells me that the stroke wasn't as severe as the last one.''

Relieved, Rhea showed Frank Masado into the living room of Joey's penthouse.

''How's my grandson?''

Before Rhea could answer, Nicci said, ''Otay, Papa.''

Rhea had never questioned why Nicci was drawn to his tough-looking grandfather. Like his sons, Frank Masado was tall and dark and showed a world of experience in the age lines on his face.

Rhea had to admit that the black eye patch Frank wore added to his overall tough-guy look, but she'd seen the gentle side of this man with Grace and Elena, had watched him on the beach with his grandson. She had heard him laugh, a rich heavy rumble that had made her stop and stare.

''Elena told me Joey stole Niccolo right out from under the noses of my guards.''

Frank's raised voice made Nicci cringe, and when Frank realized that he'd frightened his grandson, he softened his voice and reached for Nicci. ''Come to your papa, Niccolo. Let me see how big you've gotten since last I saw you.''

Rhea handed over her son.

"Daddy's room dat way, Papa.'' Nicci pointed toward the hall.

Since he had wandered into Joey's room and found his parents kissing, Nicci couldn't stop talking about his daddy's room, or the "round bed in the sky.'' He'd been complaining that he was hungry—until he spied the bed on the platform and the wall-size TV. Since then, he'd been trying to convince Rhea that he should take his afternoon nap on Daddy's bed.

"I'm on my way to see Joey,'' Frank said, "but I wanted to check on you and see how you're holding up.''

"I'm fine. We both are.''

Joey's father looked exhausted. His concern for Grace was partly responsible, but Rhea knew that Joey's actions had only added to his father's worry.

"I should have told him years ago, you know. I suppose he's blazing mad. Joey in a mood is ten times worse than Lucky backed in a corner.''

"Yesterday he was furious,'' Rhea agreed. "Today, he's…a little less unreasonable.''

"Did he tell you how he learned you and Niccolo were at Santa Palazzo?''

"No.''

"Did you mention Grace or Elena?''

"Of course not. If Joey knows about them, he

learned it from someone else, not me. I know how important it is to keep them a secret."

"Until I can get you back on a flight to Florida, don't speak to anyone. And stay inside."

Niccolo squirmed to be put down, and when Frank set him on the floor, he ran for the hall. "I go ta jus yook, Mama. I no touch nuffin. I pomis."

"He loves it here," Rhea said. "I thought he would hate it, but in one day, he acts like it's always been his home."

"Rhea, don't do that. You can't stay. This can never be home for either of you. Don't make the mistake of thinking you and Joey will ever be able to raise Niccolo together. For that to happen, Carlo Talupa's world would have to come crashing down around him. And he's too powerful for that ever to happen."

"I don't think Joey's going to agree to give up his son."

"He will, once I tell him why he must. I should have told him the truth years ago. My pride wouldn't allow it, and now the past is back, threatening all of our lives. I'm sorry about that, Rhea. Sorry you've been caught in the middle since day one."

"He never married Sophia, Frank. You should have told me."

"I thought it would be easier for you if you thought he had moved on. Sophia is his future, whether he wants her to be or not. He must realize that.''

Resigned, Rhea said, ''I know why we should go back, Frank. That doesn't make this any easier. Not now, not after Joey knows he has a son. You should see them together. They—'' She stopped herself. ''I'll go back, Frank. I will, but only with Joey's blessing. This time I won't run. I can't.''

''Joey's a lucky man, Rhea. He can never know how lucky. But your loyalty to my son makes this just that much harder.''

''It's more than loyalty, Frank.''

''I know you love him. And it's true we can't choose who we love. Just ask me. I'm an expert on forbidden love.''

''I'm not sorry,'' she said softly. ''I'm not sorry that I love Joey. I've never been sorry.''

Rhea turned away to hide her damp eyes. Seconds later, the memory of Joey's morning kiss came back to her on a wave of emotion. The kiss had been full of passion. So open and so honest that it had left her not only breathless and shaken, but with a promise that maybe someday he would be able to forgive her for keeping Nicci from him.

In one day's time, if he could go from hate to mercy, what might happen if they had more time together?

''Joey told me that Stud is in jail.''

''I intended to tell you.''

Rhea heard Frank come up behind her. She turned in time to see him digging in his pants pocket. "Here." He handed her a gun. A small .22. "Take this and hide it. Somewhere that you can get to it quickly if you have to. It's loaded. And you know how to use it. It's the one you practiced with, so it's not a stranger to you."

Rhea took the .22. Frank had insisted that she learn how to shoot a gun. How to defend herself. She had never been afraid of guns. Her ex-husband was a cop. Guns had been a part of his life.

Frank touched her cheek. "Keep alert, *figlia*. Until I can get you back to Santa Palazzo, trust no one. And remember, don't mention Grace to anyone. Or Elena. No one can know that Grace is alive, or that she and I have a daughter."

"You're an idiot, Joey."

Joey looked up from his desk to see his father charging into his office, and without hesitation he said, "And you're a lying son of a bitch, Frank."

"You should have come to me the minute you found out I had her. What were you thinking? No! Forget that. You weren't thinking at all! You could have gotten yourself and your brother killed breaking into Santa Palazzo like thieves. My men are instructed to shoot first and ask questions later. Dammit, Joey, I taught you better than that!"

"What you taught me, Frank, was to hold onto

hour, but they were expected to call me once a day and tell me where you were and what you were doing. That's how I knew from the beginning that you were interested in Rhea Williams. It was a surprise, I'll admit that. She was Stud Williams's wife and he was working for us. I thought that was a bit reckless on your part, but—"

"Ex-wife," Joey corrected.

Frank puffed on his cigar. "Yes, she was his ex, but Stud didn't see it that way. He wanted her back in his house. Divorced or not, he always saw her as his."

Joey's jaw jerked. "That might be the way Stud saw it. I saw it different."

"Rhea's a beautiful woman. But three years ago no one could have convinced me of that. You know that better than anyone. She was going through hell, and she looked like it."

Joey leaned forward, rested his elbows on his desk. "Old news, Frank. Move on."

"I had no intention of interfering. I really believed you'd have your fun with Rhea, and then settle into a life with Sophia by the end of the year, like we planned. But then you broke off your engagement, and the next thing I knew I got a call from one of my watchdogs telling me Rhea was pregnant. Of course, there was a possibility that the baby wasn't yours—that it could have been Stud Williams's child. I was hopeful, but I had to be certain. I went to see

Rhea. She was wary of me but she stood her ground. Strong women are rare, and I liked her right from the start. I understood then why she appealed to you.''

Joey sat back and rubbed his jaw as he listened.

"She confirmed my fears. She said, yes, she was pregnant. And when I asked her if you were the father, she didn't admit it right away. But I knew the minute I mentioned your name that it was your baby. And when she touched her belly and raised her chin... She was already protective of the baby, and me showing up asking questions must have been unsettling for her. When she finally admitted it, I knew what I had to do.''

Frank unbuttoned his suit jacket and spread it wide to reveal his 9-mm tucked into a leather shoulder holster. "The real pisser is, I thought I taught you better than that, Joey. I thought I was clear on the rules of the game. And one of those rules is, you can take whatever you want as long as you don't leave behind incriminating evidence. A baby is damn incriminating evidence.''

"Is there a point to this segment of your story, Frank?''

"There is. Rule two, if you don't want someone going behind you and mopping up your mess, don't leave one. And there's nothing wrong with paying for sex. Top dollar, if need be. Hell, I say have it delivered. Just keep it uncomplicated. And the most important of all is, don't help yourself to another man's property because it always goes sour in the end."

"I guess you ought to know something about that," Joey taunted. "At least I didn't steal my best friend's wife, then turn my back on her when things turned...*sour*."

Frank lunged forward. But before he could get close enough to put his hands on his son, Joey pulled an open knife from the top drawer of his desk and pointed it at his father.

"Sit down, Frank."

His father eased back onto the chair. "Okay, you're right. I wanted Grace Tandi and I took her. And I paid for it. It was a hard lesson. A lesson I thought I had passed on."

"Don't you mean, Grace paid?"

Frank swore, then left the chair and headed to the bar. He splashed scotch into a glass and quickly drained it. Glaring at Joey from across the bar, he said, "You're right. Grace paid. I ignored the rules, and she got caught in the middle. I lost my best friend, and he lost his wife."

Frank poured himself another drink. "Your mother was dead and I was alone, Joey. I took care of business, raised my sons the best I knew how, and went to bed alone. I did that for six years. A man gets lonely for a woman's touch. I'm sure you can relate to that."

"What's wrong with paying for it, and having it delivered?" Joey taunted.

"That would have been the smart thing." Frank finished off his second glass of scotch. "But like you, I was young and felt invincible. Vito and I were climbing the ladder fast at that time. Our territories were growing. Money was starting to come easy. When Vito would take Grace out for an evening, he started asking me along. Grace was a gorgeous woman. Tall and dark, with the softest brown eyes and the sweetest smile. I started looking forward to those dinners. Then I started imagining what it would be like to make love to Vito's wife."

Frank stepped around the bar and leaned against it. "It wasn't Grace's fault. I was used to getting what I wanted, and like I said, the money was coming easy. I remember feeling pretty unbeatable. One day I just decided that I wanted her, and so I took her."

"And then?"

"And then a month later, hell rose up and fried my ass. I didn't know Carlo was having me watched. One night I called Grace to meet me at a motel, and when I got there, Carlo and Vito were waiting for me. Vinnie D'Lano, too. When Grace got there, we were put in a car and driven north to Vinnie's fishing cabin. There wasn't a damn thing I could do. I tried to talk them out of what I was sure they were going to do, but Carlo only laughed. Vito…he didn't say much. He just looked like he'd been gutted.''

Frank left the bar and headed for the wall of windows behind Joey's desk. As he stared out at the skyline, he continued. ''Carlo said Grace's infidelity was a sign that Vito was weak. He said if Vito couldn't control his family, how could he control his action on the street? He said Vito would lose his respect and his influence unless he proved to everyone he wasn't afraid to right the wrong. He needed to show the *famiglia* that he wasn't a coward, Carlo said. And that meant he needed to kill Grace. The look on Vito's face—I'll never forget it.''

Joey watched his father lower his head. It was the first time Frank had ever discussed his affair with Grace Tandi. The first Joey had heard that it was Carlo Talupa who had ordered Vito to kill his wife. He asked, ''So Vito took out Grace—and what happened to you? Carlo didn't want you dead?''

''No. That's not what he wanted for me.''

''Why not?''

''Because Carlo knew Grace was important to me. To go behind Vito's back, I had to care about her. Maybe he even knew I loved her. So instead of killing me, he wanted me alive so that I would suffer every day for the rest of my life. He wanted all of the capos and soldiers to see me stripped and broken. He wanted them to know what it would cost them if they ever tried to cheat him or steal from the *famiglia.*"

There was a moment of silence, then Frank turned to face Joey. Slowly his hand drifted to the patch over his eye. "I became Carlo's walking billboard that night. Vito took my eye while Vinnie and Carlo held me down."

Joey stared at his father's patched eye. He was nine years old when his father had arrived at Lavina Ward's house to pick up him and his brother, wearing the patch. He had never said a word about what happened. A day later, when Joey had gotten up the courage to ask, he'd been told it was none of his business and never to mention it again.

"Your eye was the price?"

"Yes. For looking at another man's wife. Carlo said, the punishment fit the crime. I also lost my territory. Carlo gave it all to Vito as restitution for his loss and humiliation. And since Vinnie had gotten out of bed to help clean up my mess, he was entitled to something, too. Carlo asked him what he wanted from me, and he said he wanted my eldest son to marry his daughter when the time came. Sophia was only one year old at the time."

And what about the deal? Sophia's words, and her smug grin, came back to Joey.

Frank must have seen the disbelief on Joey's face. He said, "I didn't have a choice. And at the time I didn't think it was such a bad deal. You were nine

years old, and it would be years before you would
be expected to marry her. A lot could happen in that
time. I thought there had to be a way out of it, I just
hadn't come up with it yet. For the next several years
I watched Sophia grow up, determined to get you out
of the deal I'd made with Vinnie. Then, as she got
older, I started to convince myself that maybe it
wasn't such a bad deal. She was smart and she was
beautiful. That's when I came up with the idea to get
you to fall in love with her. I thought if you two
were together enough, you would eventually fall for
her, and then—''

"I wouldn't have to know the truth."

"Carlo and Vinnie never knew that I didn't tell
you about the deal I'd made with him. There was no
time line, so as long as you looked like you were
eventually going to fulfill the deal we'd made, no
one suspected you didn't know what was expected
of you. Then you two got engaged, and I thought
everything was going to work out. That is, until you
started seeing Rhea secretly and broke off the engagement.''

"How did you explain that to Carlo and Vinnie?"

"I told them that you were involved in a heavy
business deal that was worth millions. That it was
going to require you to be single for a while longer.
They understood what that meant. In fact, Vinnie
said he appreciated your consideration for Sophia. I
said you were still planning to marry her as soon as

One Way Out

things got settled. Vinnie's as greedy as Carlo when it comes to money. I knew if I mentioned millions, they would agree that the marriage was secondary. It bought us some time.''

''And that's when you decided to send Rhea to Santa Palazzo?''

''Once I learned she was pregnant, I couldn't chance Carlo and Vinnie finding out. Your sleeping with her would have been fine. But the child was a problem. Vinnie chose you for Sophia because he wanted the money tie. A child by you and Sophia would merge our families.'' Frank started to pace. ''It was just like I'd stepped back into the same nightmare I'd created years ago. Back then, Grace paid for my mistake, and now your son was going to pay for yours. Even though you had no idea what had transpired years earlier.'' His father stopped and leveled Joey a look. ''That's why we have to get Rhea and Niccolo back to Santa Palazzo as quick as possible.

''I'm not afraid for myself, Joey. Yes, Carlo will come after me, but Vinnie will come after you and Niccolo. Rhea, too. They will be made examples of for the good of the *famiglia*. They'll cut you, Joey. Where you'll bleed the most. And like I said, it's always the innocent who end up getting hurt.''

Joey felt like someone had ripped his guts out through a pinhole. He turned away, and this time he was the one who went to stand at the window.

Yesterday he'd been furious with his father; today he realized that even though Frank was ultimately responsible for everything that had happened, three years ago his father had rescued Rhea and Nicci from certain death. Everything was making sense now, and the reality of it all was too bizarre not to believe.

"Joey, please. Send them back. You can't protect them here. Not against Carlo."

"It's too late for that, Frank." He turned from the window. "It's too risky at this time to send them back."

"What do you mean, it's too risky? They haven't been here longer than a day. I know for a fact that Carlo's in Detroit for a few days. If no one knows they're here, we can get them back and keep Niccolo a secret."

Joey shook his head. "Last night, at least a hundred people at the Stardust saw Rhea…and my son. Included in that hundred was Sophia D'Lano. This morning she came here to see me. Not knowing anything about your deal with Carlo and Vinnie, I told her I didn't intend to marry her. She left my office making heavy threats. I figure by now, Vinnie D'Lano has made a call to Carlo with the news."

Frank collapsed onto a chair as if he'd been sucker punched. The color drained from his face. "You're right, it would be too risky to move them now. I've been able to keep Santa Palazzo a secret for twenty-four years, and if they discover that I…" Frank stopped himself from going on. "Carlo can never know that—"

"Grace is alive. Is that what you were going to say, Frank?"

When his father simply stared at him, Joey walked back to his desk and slid open his top drawer. As he hit the switch on a tape recorder, he took his chair, then watched more color drain from his father's face as the conversation he'd had with Rhea an hour earlier began to spill into the room.

After the tape had played out, Frank stated, "You bugged your penthouse."

Joey shook his head. "No. I bugged Rhea."

"How?"

"She's wearing a dime-size microphone. It's in the back pocket of her jeans. So let's start over, Frank. And this time, why don't you dig a little deeper into the past and tell me everything? Tell me how you managed to keep Grace alive, and how nine months later she gave birth to my sister. Elena, right?"

Chapter 6

"You're right. The word on the street is that Vinnie wants your balls in a jar, and Carlo wants Frank's throat slit."

Joey looked up from his desk the next morning as Lucky walked into his office. "What else?"

"How do you know there's something else?"

"There's always something else with Carlo Talupa. Let's hear it."

"He flew in late last night from Detroit. This morning he put out a contract on Frank. He's offering money and…Rhea."

Joey felt his world tilt. "Rhea…"

"That's right. He called Mickey Norelli out of Philly and Carmine Solousi in Detroit. They don't like each other ever since Carmine stole Mickey's girlfriend. Carlo's playing one against the other to get the job done faster. They also have an appetite for blondes, remember? That means we're going to have to come up with something quick.''

''Where's Frank?''

''In his suite, pacing and cussing. Did Jacky call?''

''He called. He's doing what he can on his end. What's the consensus on the street?''

''The soldiers are talking. Carlo's the boss and they know he's got the muscle to back whatever action he takes. I don't think we're going to get much support unless we can shake things up big-time.''

Joey studied the way Lucky was standing and wondered how many drinks it had taken to get his brother out of bed. Since yesterday everything had gone to hell, and there was a lot to consider. Where Lucky was concerned, he worried that Carlo would see him as an easy target. Everyone knew that since Lucky's stint in the hospital he was fighting a battle with pain.

''I know what you're thinking, *fratello*. You got plenty to deal with, without worrying about me. I can take care of myself.''

''Make me feel better and get a couple of the men to watch your back. Carlo will hurt us anywhere he can. If he plans to take over Masado Towers he'll need to get rid of you, too.''

''You know I prefer to work alone.''

''Make an exception this time.'' Joey leaned back

in his chair and watched Lucky head to the bar. "You got guards on Frank?"

"Three. I sealed off his floor. He's not happy about it, but that's the way it has to be for now." From behind the bar, Lucky looked at Joey. "I don't agree with the way Frank handled the situation twenty-four years ago. He should have told you what went down. Not right away, of course. But when you were older."

"Yes, he should have. And he should have told us about Grace, too," Joey added.

"Damn right, he should have. Still, I'm not going to let Carlo take him down. Frank screwed up, but we've all done that. He's suffered enough, *fratello*."

Joey's jaw jerked. "I still want to wring Frank's neck for taking Rhea to Santa Palazzo without telling me, but I know why he did it. Maybe that's enough for now."

Lucky uncorked the scotch. "Frank said Vito refused to kill Grace."

Joey nodded. "Frank said he passed out after they took his eye, and when he woke up, he found Grace laying beside him; she'd been beaten and her face cut. Grace was in the middle of having another stroke the other night when we arrived at Santa Palazzo to get Niccolo. That's why Rhea wasn't in her room at midnight. That was the family emergency your men reported."

"Yeah, I figured that out, too. That's why Frank flew to Florida so quickly. It was only after he ar-

rived that he learned we'd been there and taken Niccolo.''

"You never saw Grace or Elena the four days you
were there taking pictures, right?''

"No, I never did. Frank said Grace doesn't leave
the house much. So we have a sister.''

Joey detected a note of sarcasm in Lucky's voice.

He caught his brother staring, and asked, "What
are you looking at?''

Lucky carried the bottle back to Joey's desk and
hooked his hip on the corner of the desk. "Frank
told me what was on the tape. What Rhea said.''

Joey said nothing.

Lucky raised the bottle to his lips. Two swallows
later, he said, "Did you talk to her about it last night?
Did you tell her you know everything? Did you tell
her you know how she feels about you?''

Joey had been waiting for his brother to hit on that
subject. He came to his feet. "No. I haven't had time
to—''

"That's bull, Joey.''

Joey scowled at his brother. "Okay, so how do
you suggest I go about bringing it up?''

"You just come out and say it.''

"'I bugged you with a microphone, darlin'. Yesterday when you confessed that you love me, that
you've always loved me, I got it on tape.' You think
that'll work, do you?''

Lucky scratched his rugged jaw. "Women hate being manipulated. Even if it's for their own good.

They got that tunnel-vision thing going most of the time. Still, you're going to have to talk to her. Maybe if you start out telling her she's not alone…''

"Not alone?" Joey's scowl deepened.

"You saying you don't love her?"

"I never said that."

"I figure you do. Jacky thinks so, too. He says you're acting like a man struggling at both ends." Lucky's gaze dropped to his brother's crotch to drive his point home. "He says it's frustrating as hell, but once a man faces the truth, the perks are hot sex on a regular basis, buying condoms by the box instead of singles in a public rest room, and someone to wash your back in the shower."

Joey jammed his hands into his pockets and stared at his brother from the other side of the desk.

"I told Jacky I had already experienced hot sex," Lucky continued. "After all, there's a fireplace in the old house. That I'd been buying my condoms by the case, not by the box, since I was nineteen. And that my long-handled brush in the shower reached everything just fine."

"Sounds to me like you and Jacky need a new hobby besides discussing my personal life," Joey groused.

Lucky corked the scotch, slid off the desk and set the bottle in a chair, then eased himself into the one next to it. "Frank called it messy…you making a baby with Rhea. He doesn't know you like I do. You've never made a mess in your life. Not *Joe*

Cool. Not as long as I've known you. Neat as a pin,
Vina used to say. You still fold your socks together
before you throw 'em in the laundry hamper?''

"Where's this going, Lucky?''

"We're an unbeatable team, *fratello*. But only if
we level with each other. I need to know just what
we're fighting for. I need to know what you can't
live without and what is expendable before we go
any farther with this war against Carlo. I need you
to be honest with me and Jacky. Honest with yourself.''

Joey spun away from his desk. When he turned
back, he hit his chest with his fist. "Okay, she's still
renting space in here. Is that what you want to hear,
Lucky? I wish it was different, but it's not. I wanted
to hate her for lying to me, but I can't. She's been
in my head and in my—'' again, he fisted his chest
"—in here since I saw her that night at the hospital.
And now that I know she cares about—''

"Loves you,'' Lucky helped out. "She used the
word love, *fratello*.''

"Okay, Lucky! Loves me.'' Joey started over.
"Now that I know she loves me, I'm damn well going to find a way to send Carlo to hell for the misery
he's caused all of us.''

Lucky reached for the bottle of scotch. "See, that
didn't hurt too bad, did it?''

Joey nailed his brother with a black look.

"Let's drink to sending Carlo to hell.''

"I don't think so, bro.''

Lucky's hand stilled. "What now?"

"I agree I want Carlo on his knees, and I agree we're an unbeatable team…if *we* level with each other." He pointed to the bottle. "So my question to you is, how many of those did it take to get you out of bed this morning? How many to get through the day? You look like you're hurtin' bad. Just how bad, Lucky?"

"I don't need the booze to do my job, Joey, if that's the question behind the question. It makes it easier, but I don't need it. Not to shoot straight or to rip a man apart."

"Are you sure?"

Lucky slowly got to his feet. "I spoke with the doctor a week ago."

Joey was surprised to hear it. Lucky hated doctors as much as he did. Surprised, but encouraged, he said, "What did he say?"

"He tells me that my scar is crowding the blood vessels along my spine."

"Is there something that can be done?"

"Surgery."

"So have it."

"I'm considering it. But right now, taking Carlo off at the knees is more important. So what's this plan you mentioned on the phone? The one you said I wasn't going to like? Why the hell not?"

Rhea found the electronic bug in the back pocket of her jeans just before lunch. At first she had no

idea what it was. Then she remembered the gold disk
on Norman Gate's lapel and suddenly realized she'd
been played for a fool.

Faced with the truth, she now knew that yesterday's kiss, the one she had thought was so open and
honest, had been nothing more than a calculated
scheme to plant the tiny microphone.

The truth stung her pride, but she had no one to
blame but herself. She had made it easy for him. Her
confession that she'd been without a man in her life
for three years must have made it hard for him to
keep from laughing while he gathered her into his
arms to rescue her from her pathetic plight.

Yes, easy is what she'd been. She'd melted against
him, and in his arms she had remembered everything.
But more important, he had remembered, too, and
that knowledge had made it all so simple for him.
Now he not only knew how vulnerable she was with
him, but he knew why—he knew she was in love
with him, he knew about Grace, and he knew about
Elena.

She needed to call Frank, but on the heels of that
decision came the overwhelming urge to face Joey
first. And that's when she had called Opal Carvino.

In spite of her plan not to like Opal, Rhea was
more than a little impressed when the nanny came
through the door an hour later. Opal was sixty-two,
and wore her rouge a bit too high and her glasses a
bit low on her nose. But she came ready to work, her

handbag full of books to read to Nicci, and sugarless treats.

Rhea learned that Opal was a retired nurse with credentials that made her better suited to run a children's hospital than to take care of one little boy. But the best part of all was that Nicci liked her. He laughed at the older woman's enthusiasm, blushed at her praise when he'd had the courage to try a new vegetable for lunch, and had fallen asleep in her arms while she read him a story.

If Rhea wasn't so angry with Joey, she would have been able to appreciate the great pains he'd taken to find a woman of Opal's caliber in such a short time. In fact, Opal admitted that Mr. Masado had promised her a bonus if she would move out of her apartment and into a suite at Masado Towers within twenty-four hours. Opal had gladly accepted the offer, and now resided five floors below them.

"I hope to be back by dinnertime," Rhea told Opal. "But if I'm not, go ahead and feed Nicci. I've left a menu in the kitchen."

"It wasn't necessary to go to the trouble of a menu, Ms. Williams, but if it makes you feel more comfortable, I'll follow it to the letter."

"Thank you, it does," Rhea said, then went to Nicci's room to check on him. He usually napped for three hours every afternoon, and counting on that, Rhea left the penthouse focused on her mission.

Outside in the hall, she faced Norman Gates with a sweet smile pasted on her face, and told him that she needed a few things from the grocery store. Some personal items she would prefer to attend to herself. Norman hesitated, then said, ''I can't let you go unless you agree to take Murphy and Willard with you, Rhea.''

''Oh, that's no problem.'' Rhea smiled at the two men who resembled WWF wrestlers, then stepped into the elevator, shouldered between the two bullnecks.

Joey was in his office with Lucky and Jackson when he got the call from Gates that Rhea was missing, and that her bodyguards had been scrambling to locate her for twenty minutes with no luck.

Afraid that Carlo had struck hard and fast before they had gotten a chance to take action against him first, Joey sent Lucky in one direction to aid in the search and Jackson in another. Then he went to grill Gates on the chain of events that had led to Rhea's disappearance.

There had been no mention of Niccolo, and knowing how protective Rhea was of their son, he was surprised to find Opal Carvino in his home, knitting beside the bed while his son took his afternoon nap.

The discovery of Opal explained why Rhea had felt comfortable leaving the penthouse, but not what had motivated her to do so. That is, until Joey spied the glass of scotch on the bar with the miniature microphone settled on the bottom.

It took him another hour and a half, and fifty-four

men tearing Masado Towers apart, before Lucky
called and told him to meet him in front of the Stardust. When Joey stepped off the elevator he was expecting to see Rhea with his brother, but the only
one waiting for him was Lucky, wearing a heavy
scowl.

"Where is she?" Joey demanded. "I thought you
said two of the men found her."

"They thought they had her. But it's not her."

"What do you mean it's not her?"

Lucky motioned to the woman who had been de-
tained by his two men in the corridor. "Blond, beautiful, wearing jeans and a black sweater. That's the
description Gates gave us. I don't have to say more,
do I?"

Joey eyed the pretty blonde wearing jeans and a
black sweater. "*Maledizione!* Pay her off and get that
picture you took of Rhea in Florida blown up and
circulated so the men know who the hell they're
looking for."

"I'll get right on it."

Joey rode the elevator down to the lobby with
Lucky. He wanted to believe that Rhea wouldn't do
something stupid, but he couldn't be sure, and that's
what was bothering him the most. Frank had told him
that she was well aware of the danger she and Niccolo were in, and yet she had left the protection of
the penthouse and his men. Why? What was she
up to?

It was after Lucky had left to retrieve Rhea's

photo, and Joey was contemplating his next move, that he noticed a woman wearing a black sweater leave the front doors of Silks and head for the elevator corridor.

He turned to study the woman, whose black hat hid her eyes as well as her hair. He was sure that he had lost his mind thinking it might be Rhea, until he began to study the woman's walk. And that wasn't hard to do, the way the short black skirt showed off a beautiful pair of long legs and a magnificent behind.

After a few seconds of watching, Joey swore, then punched in a number on his cell phone as he slipped into the crowd to follow the lovely behind. "Lucky, call off the dogs. I've got her."

His cell phone back in his pocket, Joey picked up the pace, as Rhea headed for an elevator; she looked like one of the hundreds of women who daily shopped the boutiques at Masado Towers. He stepped into the elevator along with a half dozen women loaded down with colorful shopping bags, aware that Rhea was trying hard to keep herself hidden behind a large woman who carried a purse the size of a Volkswagen.

One by one, the women exited the elevator over the next four stops, the last climbing off at the fourteenth floor, and leaving Rhea in the corner with her head lowered.

He noticed that the next stop was the twenty-second floor. Why Rhea had chosen that floor, he had no idea, but it really didn't matter. As soon as the elevator took off, he reached out and hit the stop button on the panel.

Arms crossed over his chest, he leaned against the wall and waited. Waited until she lifted her head before he said, "Nice outfit."

She pulled off the brimmed hat, letting her white-blond hair fall forward into her sapphire eyes. She shook her head, shoved the mass away from her face, then looked at him, her expressive eyes telling him she definitely had something on her mind, as well as a reason behind her little afternoon escapade.

"What gave me away?" she finally asked.

"The black sweater choking your neck." Joey wasn't about to mention the rest. It was the walk that had convinced him it was her. That, and the fact that he'd put her legs to memory three years ago.

"Two hours and—" she glanced at her watch "—sixteen minutes. I guess your security system and your *assistants* aren't infallible."

"That's what this is all about? Testing my security?"

She flashed him a look, part hurt, part anger. "You have to admit their performance today brings up a number of questions. Do they have what it takes? Can you really protect your son as well as you think you can?" She shrugged. "Should I go on?"

Joey's jaw jerked.

"I guess more doesn't always mean better. How many men are out searching for me, Joey?"

"That was your objective? To bring my attention to the weak links in my organization?"

She didn't answer.

Joey shook his head. "It's an interesting theory, but I don't think that's why you're out to jerk my chain today. No, I think it has more to do with that little gold microphone floating in the scotch glass upstairs." He saw her stiffen, and he knew he was right.

"If you wanted information, you should have come right out and asked, Joey."

"And you would have told me...everything? All I had to do was ask?"

Silence.

"I won't tolerate secrets, Rhea. My house, my rules, remember? I planted that bug yesterday morning for a reason. I can't protect what's mine if I don't know who my enemies are. If you continue to keep secrets, you're going to have to get used to finding bugs in your pockets, darlin'. I do what I have to. I won't apologize for how I live, or what I have to do to stay alive. The bottom line is to keep breathing, remember?"

She hiked her chin. "We were breathing fine at Santa Palazzo. Why not send us back?"

"It's not that simple. Maybe if I had known the reason why you were there in the first place, I would have done things different. Fact is, you're here now, and the wrong people know it. It's too dangerous to send you back."

"It's just as dangerous for us here, Joey."

"I'm glad you realize that. So, no more stunts like this one you pulled today, darlin'. *Capiche?*" Joey shoved away from the wall and reached for the bag she held. She gave it up without a fight, and he opened it to find a pair of jeans inside, flat leather shoes and a small red bag from Silks. So she'd left the penthouse in jeans, with the idea of altering her appearance once she'd ditched his guards. He looked up.

"Say it, Rhea. 'I agree there will be no more silly stunts. No more running off and scaring the hell out of me.'"

"Joey Masado scared? I don't think so."

He set the black bag down and reached inside for the package from Silks. "What's in here?"

"It's personal. Nothing you need to concern yourself with."

When he attempted to open the bag, she dropped her hat and made a grab for it. The bag ripped and the contents spilled onto the floor—a half dozen pair of sexy panties, and a black satin chemise.

She swore at him, then moved away from the wall to rescue her underwear. He'd been itching to get his hands on her all day, ever since he had admitted to himself and Lucky that Rhea's confession wasn't one-sided.

As she bent down, he wrapped his arm around her waist and pulled her up against him. As he backed her into the corner, he said, "Did you mean it?"

"Let go, Joey."

"Did you mean it?"

She dodged his eyes. "I don't know what you're talking about."

"Sure you do, otherwise you wouldn't be trying so damn hard to avoid looking at me." He gripped her chin and forced her head back so she would have to look at him. Still not willing to make eye contact with him, she closed her eyes. "Maybe you can't look at me because it makes you remember too damn much. Is that it, Rhea? Are you remembering what it felt like when I came inside you three years ago? Do you remember how you begged for it? Begged for my mouth and my tongue. Yesterday you remembered, didn't you, darlin'?"

"Let me go, Joey."

He settled his weight around her with no intention of letting her go anywhere. He would have chosen somewhere else to talk about this, but she'd picked the place, not him.

She squirmed against him, sending enough heat-filled friction over his crotch and down the front of his legs to make him swear and groan at the same time.

"I want to hear you say it. Tell me what you told Frank yesterday."

"You already know what I told Frank. Why say it again? So you can have an excuse to take more from me?"

"I don't need an excuse to take what's already mine."

She swore at him, then tried to get her knee up.

This time Joey was ready for that, and he slid his hand down her thigh and gripped her leg just above the knee. Jerking her knee to the side, he slid his leg between her thighs, then curled his fingers along the seams of the tight black skirt and yanked it up.

"Joey, no! Not here!" She renewed her fight.

"*Si*, right here. Right now."

He lowered his head and kissed her hard, driving his tongue between her teeth and into the heat of her mouth. And in that instant, she stopped struggling. Seconds later he heard the moan, the one that told him she was his.

Quickly, he slid his hands up her body to cradle her head and soften his kiss. She responded by whimpering and arching against him. Then she moved her hands inside his suit jacket to slide her arms around his waist.

The knowledge that she wanted him—*loved him*—had Joey on a mission. Groaning, he settled his hands back on her thighs. Slower this time, he hiked up her skirt, then lifted his knee until it made contact with her heat. The action spread her legs wider, forced her skirt higher.

A few more tugs and the skirt was bunched around her waist. Joey's hands slid over her backside to bring her more fully against his knee. The act teased another moan from her, and she clung to him until they were both breathing heavily.

He stepped back and looked into her stormy blue eyes. "You know what's going to happen, don't you? What has to happen."

"Yes."

He kissed her again, then his gaze drifted down her body to her lavender panties. Cut high on her hips, they made her legs look like they went on forever, and he ached to feel those shapely legs wrapped around him.

Their destination set, he leaned in and took her lips once more. He wanted to linger, to feast on her delicious mouth for hours, to take his time—but there was no time. They had already been in the elevator too long, and his men would be scrambling to find out why it had stalled between the sixteenth and seventeenth floor.

He thought about calling Gates, but there was no time for that, either. Rhea was ready for him and he was past ready. He bent his knees and kissed her belly. His fingers slid around her hips and he hooked his thumbs into the elastic of her panties and pulled them down past her sexy knees. Hungry for her, he brushed his lips over her, then dipped into her center, stroking his tongue against her until she was writhing on the wall and arching for him.

The scent of her desire drove him wild, and he moved on her again and again, his mouth sucking

Get FREE BOOKS and a FREE GIFT when you play the...

LAS VEGAS

GAME

7

Just scratch off the gold box with a coin. Then check below to see the gifts you get!

YES! I have scratched off the gold Box. Please send me my **2 FREE BOOKS** and **gift for which I qualify**. I understand that I am under no obligation to purchase any books as explained on the back of this card.

345 SDL DUYH   245 SDL DUYX

FIRST NAME

LAST NAME

ADDRESS

APT.#	CITY

(S-IM-03/03)

STATE/PROV.	ZIP/POSTAL CODE

7 7 7	Worth TWO FREE BOOKS plus a BONUS Mystery Gift!
🍒 🍒 🍒	Worth TWO FREE BOOKS!
🔔 🔔 ♣	TRY AGAIN!

Offer limited to one per household and not valid to current Silhouette Intimate Moments® subscribers. All orders subject to approval.

The Silhouette Reader Service™ — Here's how it works:

Accepting your 2 free books and mystery gift places you under no obligation to buy anything. You may keep the books and gift and return the shipping statement marked "cancel." If you do not cancel, about a month later we'll send you 6 additional books and bill you just $3.99 each in the U.S., or $4.74 each in Canada, plus 25¢ shipping & handling per book and applicable taxes if any.* That's the complete price and — compared to cover prices of $4.75 each in the U.S. and $5.75 each in Canada — it's quite a bargain! You may cancel at any time, but if you choose to continue, every month we'll send you 6 more books, which you may either purchase at the discount price or return to us and cancel your subscription.

*Terms and prices subject to change without notice. Sales tax applicable in N.Y. Canadian residents will be charged applicable provincial taxes and GST. Credit or Debit balances in a customer's account(s) may be offset by any other outstanding balance owed by or to the customer.

BUSINESS REPLY MAIL

FIRST-CLASS MAIL   PERMIT NO. 717-003   BUFFALO, NY

POSTAGE WILL BE PAID BY ADDRESSEE

SILHOUETTE READER SERVICE
3010 WALDEN AVE
PO BOX 1867
BUFFALO NY 14240-9952

NO POSTAGE
NECESSARY
IF MAILED
IN THE
UNITED STATES

and his tongue stroking until he felt her fingers in his hair, heard her little cries of ecstasy.

He backed off to touch her with his hands, to thread his fingers through her blond triangle of curls, then dipped inside.

She gasped. Arched. Clung to him.

Sensing how ready she was for him, Joey quickly came to his feet. He felt her hand brush over the front of his pants, and her desire to touch him nearly undid him. He loosened his belt, then unzipped his pants, while she bent down, shoved her panties past her ankles and stepped out of them. On the way back up, her hand slid into his pants and she cupped his sac through his underwear and squeezed.

Joey heard himself groan when she slid her fingers upward, running the heel of her hand over his thick shaft. "*Si*…that's good. So damn good," he muttered, then reached for her. No longer able to wait, he clasped her around the waist, cupped her lovely bottom and stepped closer into the corner to rest her shoulders against the wall. "Bend your knees, darlin', and curl yourself around me," he whispered.

Overdue to be sheathed inside her, the minute she did as he asked, he sent his pulsing length into her, impaling her harder than he had intended. She cried out, then buried her face against his neck to muffle her cries of rising passion.

When her body began to convulse and stretch, she moaned and settled around him. The pleasure of it all tugged him deeper, and as a delicious heat ex-

ploded around him, Joey bucked his hips and began
to set a rhythm.

The scent of her filled his nostrils, and he closed
his eyes and let himself get lost in the craving he'd
had for her ever since he'd first seen her at the hospital.

Unable to ever get enough—that was what he had
thought years ago. And now, that feeling was back.
He gripped her bottom and pumped faster. Deeper.
She panted and strained, and clung to him as she took
his hard thrusts. Seconds later, she came over him in
a series of violet spasms, her ragged cry sending him
rushing to meet her in a savage climax that nearly
took him to his knees.

At first Rhea thought the ringing was just in her
ears, but as soon as Joey swore, she came out of her
euphoric fog and realized it was some kind of alarm.

She lifted her head and saw a light flashing on the
elevator panel. "Joey…"

"That's us. Come on. We've got to get you put
back together before we get company."

Rhea unwrapped her legs from around him as he
eased out of her. She was glad for the wall at her
back when her feet touched the floor. Leaning against
it, she felt shaky and spent, but there was no time to
bask in the moment.

Focused on what she needed to do before the elevator doors opened, she accepted the handkerchief
Joey thrust into her hand. Her cheeks would have

shown her embarrassment if they weren't already full of color.

She turned away to use the handkerchief, then yanked the tight black skirt over her hips, then wrapped the evidence of her wild behavior into a ball and buried it in her fist.

When she turned back, she found Joey leaning against the opposite wall, holding her hat and watching her. To her annoyance, she realized that no one ever would have guessed by looking at him that he'd just participated in a record-breaking round of elevator sex. His clothes had been restored to perfection, and his expression was as cool as his eyes.

The bell was still ringing, and the light on the panel was still flashing.

"Ready?"

No, she wasn't ready. How could he think she was ready?

"Rhea…"

She lifted her chin, then held out her hand for her hat.

He handed her the wide-brimmed black hat, and she took it, but she didn't put it on—she would regret that later.

He reached for the panel and pushed a button. The bell stopped ringing immediately, and after the flashing light blinked twice, the elevator took off.

Seventeen.

Eighteen.

Nineteen.

Rhea suddenly remembered she wasn't wearing her underwear. She began to scan the floor, frantic to find her panties. She would die if she left them behind. Besides, she was naked beneath her skirt. She couldn't very well leave the elevator wearing no underwear.

The elevator slowed.

Twenty.

Twenty-one.

Joey took hold of her arm and pulled her toward him just as the doors began to open. His hot mouth grazing her ear, he whispered, "They're in the bag." Then the doors opened, and Rhea found herself staring into the scowling faces of over a dozen bull-necked bodyguards disguised as businessmen, each with one hand inside his suit jacket.

Rhea didn't think she would be able to move without falling on her face. Her knees felt weak and she wasn't used to high heels. But she knew she couldn't just stand there looking like a dazed fool, giving Joey's men time to consider what had been keeping them between floors for ten minutes.

Hoping her legs held her up, she took a step, then another, until she was past the collected men and their questioning eyes.

She saw Lucky, saw him motion for her to come to him where he stood beside the glass elevator. The elevator that would take her to the penthouse. She had never imagined that she would be relieved to see

Joey's brother, but just now she was, and she headed for him as quickly as her shaky legs would go.

She felt Joey's hand reaching for hers a second later, and in an instant he'd uncurled her fingers from around the white rumpled handkerchief and buried the evidence of their union deep in his pocket.

Rhea studied the elevator, wishing it were made of steel instead of glass. She wanted to disappear from sight, the sooner the better. She heard Lucky whisper something to Joey. His reaction to what his brother had said was to swear crudely. She entered the elevator, and as she turned she found Norman Gates stepping in behind her. His usual smile was gone, and he was carrying her shopping bag.

Joey glanced at her briefly, and she managed to keep her breathing steady. Then he turned, nailing the guards still standing in the wings with a kick-ass glare. It was followed by ''All of you, come with me. The security around here is unacceptable. We're going to fix it, even if it takes all day and all night.''

Chapter 7

When Vito saw Summ come through his bedroom door carrying her teapot on a tray, along with the familiar brown cup he'd grown to hate, he said, "Not tonight, witch. I'm not drinking that bitter swill tonight."

Undaunted by his gruff voice, she tossed her head and kept coming. Her hair was down and the scent of jasmine drifted to him where he lay on the bed. As sick as he was, his body reacted to the sight of her, the sway of her hips and the way her small breasts swelled the front of her silk robe.

She was good at reading his thoughts, he knew. She set the tray down on the table next to his bed, her robe parting to allow him a glimpse of her slender legs. "I have a letter for you," she said. "Sip tea, *okii Shujin,* while you read, then I will rub your feet, and take you away from your pain. Then you will rest comfortably for the night.''

Damn he liked it when she called him "big master." He shoved his rotund body upward, resting his back against the massive carved Asian headboard depicting a scene of fighting jaguars. Summ handed him the letter, then poured the tea. The letter was already open, but not read. Summ never overstepped her position when it came to his privacy. As he glanced at the familiar handwriting, his already ill mood took a nosedive. Not in any hurry to read what Carlo had to say, he stalled, content to watch Summ as she lit the candles that circled the room.

She had told him once that the candles would light the way on his journey. That whenever the time came, day or night, they would guide him down his chosen path. He wasn't sure if Summ was worried that the stairway to hell would be too dark for him to find his way, or if she was afraid cloud cover would darken the pearly gates. He believed the former, though they had never discussed his fate except to acknowledge that he would be taking a journey.

"Sip tea, *Shujin,* it will give you strength."

Keep him hard for longer than three minutes is what she meant. Vito wet his lips, anticipating the bitter taste, anticipating what would follow if he could manage to get down more than one cup of the sour crap. There are rewards in suffering the taste, she had once teased, and she had been right the one night he'd managed to empty the entire teapot.

He glanced at her and the smile appearing on her small wise face. Then she dropped her silk robe and walked naked to the stone steps that led to his indoor pool, where warm fragrant water awaited her surrounded by a herb and floral garden—a garden she ritually attended as dutifully as she did him.

Chansu's perch was there, among the fragment vetiver grass and sweet-smelling jasmine. The parrot made a chirping noise, and Summ stopped to speak to him and stroke the bird's blue head, before she entered the water with the grace of a woodland fairy.

Vito finally unfolded the letter and began to sip the Matcha and read. From time to time he would look up to watch Summ bathe. By the time he came to the bottom of the letter, he was swearing. "The bastard is threatening a nursing home," he roared. "If I don't die soon, he says he's going to remove me from my house." Vito tossed the letter into the air. "Carlo Talupa has gone too far. He needs a meat cleaver to his skinny neck."

He wasn't sure when Summ left the water, but suddenly she was beside him, again wrapped in her robe, handing him the brown cup. "Drink tea."

He accepted the cup. "I'm not dead yet," he growled.

"No, *Shujin,* not yet. Drink tea."

He took a swallow. "I still have my brain," he groused.

"More than a brain to nourish. Drink tea."

Vito drained the cup, and when she poured it full once more, he emptied that, too, then pointed to the teapot for her to refill the cup again. "You could have waited until tomorrow to show me that damn letter, Summ. I would have slept better."

"You will sleep," she assured, emptying the last of the tea from the pot into his cup. "It isn't my place to keep such things from you," she said softly. She handed him the Matcha. "I promise you will sleep well, *Shujin*."

Vito looked deeper into Summ's eyes. "But it's your place to get me roaring mad so that I'll drink your damn tea, hmm?"

A slight smile curved her lovely pink lips. "As you say, you are not dead yet. Your pleasure is also mine. Our time is short together. We must make the most of it."

She stood then and slipped out of her robe. Only this time, she was close enough for him to reach out and touch her, and for her to touch him.

"See, the tea is working already, *okii Shujin*."

It was late when Joey returned to the penthouse. After Rhea had eluded his guard for over two hours, he'd spent the rest of the day tightening security.

The living room was dark, except for the night-lights Rhea had strategically positioned along the walls. As he made his way down the hall noticing more night-lights, he stripped off his tie and unbuttoned his shirt.

He went room to room, starting with Niccolo's bedroom first, before he found Rhea and his son asleep on his bed in front of the window, the drapes open, their bodies positioned as if they had been surveying the city lights. The sight of them there, on his bed, stopped him. He had always liked kids, but to have one of his own, to have created a child with Rhea... It was an overwhelming feeling he couldn't put into words, and the mix of emotions made him feel more possessive and more resolute in his need to right the wrong that had been done to his family.

He was careful not to make any noise as he removed his suit jacket, but suddenly Niccolo sat up and looked at him. Quickly, Joey brought his finger to his lips, and his son grinned, slipped out from under a soft red blanket and crawled off the bed.

The boy was wearing his pajamas, and he carefully took the steps one at a time, his teddy bear in his hand. He toddled to Joey, who then scooped him up. Niccolo openly kissed Joey's cheek, then whispered, "Mama seeping Daddy? Shhh..."

"You should be sleeping, too," Joey acknowledged quietly.

"Me hun-wey, Daddy."

Joey carried Niccolo into the hall, leaving the door open slightly. "I'm hungry, too. Let's go see what we can find in the kitchen. Should we?"

Niccolo's brown eyes widened, and he happily

nodded in agreement. "Otay. Papa gives me piggy wides. Do you know how ta do dat, Daddy?"

Niccolo's question surprised Joey. Frank had never been interested in crazy fun. The Masado boys had grown up with a father who seldom smiled and who had never made a joke. Not that Joey remembered.

"Dats otay if you don't know how, Daddy."

Joey blinked out of his musing, then carefully slid his son onto his back, making sure that his arms remained secure around his neck. "You hanging on tight?"

"Weally tight, Daddy. Papa says I hafta."

They left the hall and entered the kitchen, then took a long route around the living room twice and into the dining room, then through the kitchen and into the breakfast nook, than back into the kitchen.

While Nicci was still giggling, Joey eased him off his back and onto the counter, then started raiding the refrigerator and the cupboards.

It was an hour later, while they were in the midst of eating peanut butter and jelly on crackers and drinking chocolate milk—Joey seated beside his son on the counter, shirtless—that Rhea entered the kitchen.

She was sleepy-eyed, her hair tousled, in her black satin robe, the one that made her look exotic and made Joey think of hot sex.

"Hi, darlin'," he said, then raised his cracker, dripping with raspberry jam. "**Hungry?**"

She studied the cracker, then Niccolo. "How many of those has he eaten, Joey?"

Joey shrugged, glanced at his son. "What are we up to, *figlio?*"

Grinning, Niccolo held up two fingers.

Joey glanced at the empty box of crackers, then the newly opened one. "I guess we had a late-night craving." He shifted his gaze back to Rhea, and he let his eyes travel over her breasts to her narrow waist where she'd belted the black robe. "Niccolo has discovered peanut butter."

She studied the jars on the counter. The jam jar was lying on its side. "I hope that jar wasn't full."

"That one was." Joey pointed to the cupboard that held the garbage. "But the one in there was only half full."

"A jar and a half of jam, plus peanut butter? You fed all of that to a two-year-old?"

"I had some." Joey checked his wristwatch. It was after eleven o'clock. "We've only been at it for a little over an hour. A good thing we didn't start any earlier or we would have had to send Gates to the grocery store."

Niccolo suddenly reached out, swiped the cracker out of Joey's hand and shoved the whole thing into his mouth. Throwing his head back, he laughed wildly, spewing cracker crumbs across the room in his mother's direction.

"Nicci! That's enough." Rhea left the doorway and started toward them. "That is not the way we eat. And you know sugar isn't a legal bedtime snack.''

''Legal?'' Joey schooled his grin, but when he saw his son start to hang his head, he realized Rhea was dead serious. Feeling responsible and wanting to rescue Niccolo, he nudged him with his arm, then leaned over and whispered in the boy's ear. When Niccolo started to laugh, Joey angled his head to see that Rhea had stopped and now stood with her hands planted on her hips.

''I think it's time for bed, mister.''

Joey could no longer keep a straight face. Grinning, he said, ''Whatever you say, darlin'.

Niccolo said, ''Bed suuucks.''

''Nicci that isn't a nice word. Don't use it again.''

''Uncle Yucky says it all the time, Mama. He says shudup, too.''

Rhea crossed the room and scooped Niccolo off the counter, then gave Joey a glare, daring him to intervene this time. Niccolo pushed back and tried to wiggle out of her arms.

''I want Daddy.''

''Nicci, stop it.''

''I want anover piggy wide.''

Niccolo threw himself back and reached for Joey's neck. The action tipped Rhea off balance, and Joey instinctively grabbed her and pulled her between his legs to steady her, his hands slipping around her waist. To Niccolo, he said, ''No more, *figlio* You could have made Mama fall.''

Niccolo looked contrite, but still he hung onto Joey's neck, keeping the three of them close. Suddenly, he grinned, mischief in his dark eyes. "Feed Mama, Daddy."

"Nicci, no. I don't want—"

"Peeeease…"

Joey studied Rhea's set jaw. "Come on, darlin'. Just one." When Niccolo let go of his neck, Joey reached into the box for a cracker.

"This is silly, Joey. I'm not hungry," Rhea protested.

Joey smeared the cracker with peanut butter, then drizzled jam on top, all the while keeping Rhea pinned between his legs.

"I mean it, Joey. I don't want any."

Joey studied Rhea's pretty mouth, and as Niccolo looked on and Rhea continued to reject the idea, he steered the cracker toward her.

"Joey…"

"Open up, darlin'."

"Peeeease, Mama."

With a sigh, she opened her mouth and Joey slid the cracker halfway in. She bit down, and as she munched on the cracker she took hold of his wrist and directed the other half into Niccolo's mouth.

Moments later, she said, "You realize, don't you, he's not going to fall asleep for hours?"

"Da-gon story. Da-gon story. Peeeease, Mama."

She arched a beautiful brow at Joey and gave him

an I-told-you-so look. "We're going to be up all night. Good going…Daddy."

As it turned out, they were up only half the night. Nicci fell asleep three hours later. Joey had managed to hang in there with her, but Rhea had told him it wasn't necessary. As she closed the door, he clasped her hand and started to pull her down the hall.

Rhea pulled back. "Joey, it's late."

"Up all night, remember? I'm game."

"You know what I meant," she protested.

His sexy dark eyes swept over her. "Tell you what I'll do. I'll let you go if I can't convince you it'll be worth it in—" he glanced at his watch "—three minutes." He punctuated the offer with a lazy kiss.

Rhea didn't remember how she'd gotten from the hall into his bedroom after that. The next thing she knew, her back was against the door and Joey was leaning forward to kiss her again.

"Joey, wait."

Softly, against her lips, he whispered, "I'm sorry about feeding Niccolo too much sugar." He reached for the ties to her robe and slipped the knot free. Sliding his hands inside, he said, "I've been wanting you to touch me for hours. Put your hands on me, darlin'. Touch me like you did this afternoon."

"Joey, it's late."

"Nicci will sleep until noon. We can, too."

Rhea had been avoiding his eyes ever since they left the kitchen, but now she could no longer keep her eyes, or her hands, off him. Reaching out, she pressed her palms against his flat abdomen and slid them upward.

"About this afternoon. You were right," she whispered.

"What was I right about?"

Rhea angled her head as he began to kiss his way down her neck. "It was a reckless thing to do," she managed to say. "Ah…making your staff turn the Towers upside down looking for me."

"*Si*, it was reckless." He peeled the robe off her shoulder. "It did have a happy ending, though. I was happy. You?"

"Yes."

Rhea sucked in her breath when his hand slid over her flat stomach and between her legs. "I didn't hurt you this afternoon, did I?"

"No."

He lowered his head and sniffed at the side of her neck. "My home is starting to smell like you, darlin'. Sweet and spicy. I like that."

He was wrong about that. His home, at least this room, smelled like him. That's why when Nicci had begged to fall asleep on Daddy's bed, she had given in to him. Secretly, she'd been aching to lie on Joey's bed and soak up his scent. To stare out the window and experience what he experienced, night after night as the city lights danced on the ceiling.

"Joey…what did you whisper to Nicci in the kitchen?"

"I told him his *madre* was pretty, even when she was mad and breathing fire like Purple Pete."

"Purple Pete?" Rhea shoved at his shoulders and he stopped kissing her neck and raised his head. "Who's Purple Pete?"

"The dragon in my bedtime story." He kissed her gently. "Sleep with me?"

Rhea's gaze traveled to the bed. "I—"

He pulled her away from the door and into his arms. As he kissed her with more assertion, Rhea gave in and wrapped her arms around his neck. The minute she offered him her open mouth, he groaned out his approval, then lifted her into his arms and carried her up the stairs to the bed. In front of the window, he let her slide down his body, then kissed her once more. Too weak to move when he stepped away from her, Rhea watched as he drew back the black velvet coverlet to reveal dark red satin sheets.

The image of Joey lying naked on the satin sheet surfaced in a flood of desire. The vision that followed was of Rhea joining him. Their naked bodies entwined together jolted her, and she instinctively pulled her robe around herself and turned away. As she stared out the window, she felt Joey wrap his arms around her and draw her against him. Gently, he nudged her head to the side, his mouth trailing kisses down her neck. She felt his hands slide over her hips. Felt his fingers curl around hers and slowly wrest her fingers from the robe's edges.

"Joey..."

"Shh…" His hands parted her robe and slipped inside. "I want to touch you, darlin'."

His hands were gentle and unhurried as they drifted over the black chemise, then slid underneath. He caressed and stroked her rib cage, then started upward. One hand took the lead and slid between her breasts, then across the swell of her right breast.

He said, "You have to tell me if there's a possibility that I could hurt you. If there's pain or something I need to know."

There was concern in his voice, and Rhea knew that if she turned to look at him, she would see that same concern in his eyes. She said, "There's no pain, Joey. Just a terrible scar. A scar I don't want you to see. Please, Joey."

"It's all right, darlin'. I've seen lots of scars."

"I don't want you to see this one," she insisted.

She was almost ready to pull away, when he said, "Okay."

Rhea let out a relieved sigh. Then just as quickly tensed as both of his hands moved over her breasts, raising the satin by half. His hands rolled over her fullness, his thumbs finding her nipples.

"I always wanted to touch you here," he whispered against her ear. "The bandages prevented that. I used to imagine what you would feel like when they came off."

His admission, and the way he was touching her as if she were made of glass, had Rhea arching into his hands and closing her eyes. "Do I feel like you imagined?"

"Mmm…better."

His voice had turned husky, and Rhea suddenly held her breath as his fingers followed the line that marred her flesh. The scar started next to her nipple and moved outward across the swell of her breast. Once it reached her rib cage, it curved upward and followed the entire outer width.

She had worked with special creams to diminish the scar's redness. Now all that remained was a vivid white line.

His hot breath on her neck sent another wave of longing between Rhea's legs, made her nipples ache. Shivering, heart pounding, she again arched her back.

"You like me touching you, don't you? After you left town, I thought I had imagined that."

While his right hand divided its time between her breasts, his left hand slid over her belly and into her panties. Cupping her silky triangle, he curved his fingers and delved into her moist heat.

"Spread your legs," he whispered. "I want to feel how wet you are."

He stroked and fondled her until Rhea's heart was racing and she was panting. Suddenly, he swept her robe off her shoulders and turned her to face him. Fully aroused now, Rhea curled into him, anxious to know his body again.

She kissed him and stroked his bare chest. Her fingers worked open his belt and unzipped his pants.

She'd never been aggressive sexually. Early in her marriage to Stud, he had made her afraid, and she'd become frigid. He had accused her of being cold and unfeeling, and she had thought that maybe he was right. Then Joey had entered her life, and the fear had melted away. With him, she had felt only hot. Starved.

Everything had been different with Joey. She couldn't explain why. All she knew was that from the beginning he'd set her on fire, both emotionally and physically.

She slid her hand into his pants and moved her fingers over him until he was a piece of stone in her hand. She continued to stroke him while they kissed, his tongue pushing past her teeth to taste her. She made a little hungry noise in the back of her throat when his hands moved to her backside to fondle her.

They were both panting and moaning when he abruptly broke free. Quickly he sent his pants and shorts to the floor, then said, "Take off your panties."

Rhea did as he asked, sliding the black panties down her thighs and past her knees. When she stepped out of them and looked up, Joey was sitting on the edge of the bed, watching her. She came to him, wearing her black chemise and nothing else, knowing his eyes were locked on the visible silky blond curls between her legs.

A moan ripped through him as he reached for her

and swept her onto the bed. He rolled with her, and she was suddenly beneath his muscular body.

Kissing her hard and fast, he said, "I don't want to rush this. Not like this afternoon."

Rhea said, "Let me be on top. Let me straddle you."

She had never uttered those words before—had never ridden. When they had been together three years ago, she had barely been able to move. The sex they had shared had been restrained and agonizingly slow.

She ached to move with him, to touch him and slide her body over him. To be his equal.

He cupped her satin-covered breasts. Lightly brushing his fingers over her aroused nipples, he smiled, then said, "So the lady likes to ride, does she?"

Rhea blushed. "You said you didn't want to rush. I thought maybe if I—"

He lowered his head, his lips finding first one breast, then the other. Through the satin, he teased and sucked until the chemise clung to her and outlined her nipples. "I don't want to rush, but I need to be inside you," he whispered, then slid forward and started into her. "I remember the look on your face that first time. The way you came... I've never been able to forget it. It was like I was the first for you. The only man who had—"

He stopped moving. Rhea was sure it was because

he had felt her stiffen, and why he was suddenly looking at her with questioning eyes.

"That's it, isn't it. Why I couldn't forget any of it. It was the first time for you, wasn't it?"

Yesterday he had taped her confessing to Frank that she loved him. Minutes ago, he'd touched her scars. For him to discover that he was the single force behind her womanhood was simply too much. Rhea tried to break free, but it only served to set his body on course once again, and he began to sink into her.

The look in his eyes told her there was no use denying it. He knew he was the only man who had ever sent her body soaring. Unable to remove herself in body, she closed her eyes and turned her head. Without warning, he gripped her waist, then rolled onto his back and set her astride him. Still inside her, he fastened his hands around her waist and arched his hips to keep her seated on his pulsing erection.

"Joey…"

A primitive moan erupted from somewhere deep inside him, and he muttered, "Take me, darlin'. Ride me."

He was in as much need as she was, Rhea realized, and she relaxed her hips, the act driving him deeper inside her. As the air left his lungs, another moan surfaced from the depths of him.

Rhea could feel him swelling inside her, and she leaned forward and kissed him. Having learned from him, she swept her tongue into his mouth to taste him.

The fact that she was seducing him and he was letting her magnified her desire, and as she began to ride him harder, she realized it was quite possible that this was the first time Joey Masado had ever surrendered any part of himself to anyone.

Joey felt a warm hand move over his chest, and he smiled and blinked awake. Ready to roll Rhea to her back and bury himself inside her, he was startled to see his son sitting beside him holding his bear.

Grinning down at him, Niccolo removed his hand from Joey's chest and replaced it with his bear. "Mama's in da baffroom. Nana's in da kitchen sweeping cwumms. She says der evywhere."

Joey sat up and glanced at the clock. It was after twelve, and he couldn't believe that he'd slept the entire morning away. Suddenly it registered that he was supposed to meet Jackson and Lucky in his office at one o'clock.

"Nicci! If you've woken up your father, your mother is going to be angry."

Both Joey and Niccolo looked toward the partially closed door. It was Opal Carvino's voice coming from the hall. Niccolo's grin disappeared. He looked back at his father, his eyes indicating he was in trouble.

Joey winked, then smiled. "It's okay. We'll tell Mama I was already awake."

"Nicci? Come out here right now."

"Otay, Nana." Niccolo grabbed his bear, scooted

off the bed and headed for the door. Just before he slipped out to face Opal, he turned and waved at his father.

When the door closed, Joey climbed out of bed and headed for the bathroom. Naked, he opened the door and stepped inside. The shower was running, and his eyes locked on Rhea's silhouette inside the large glassed-in cylinder shower.

Anxious to keep his appointment with Lucky and Jackson, he crossed the room and opened the door. But as he stepped inside, he remembered Rhea's reluctance last night to reveal her scars to him. She was beneath the shower spray and her eyes were closed. She raised her arms to rinse the shampoo from her hair, and in that split second, he saw the vivid scar that marred her right breast.

The scar traveled from the right side of her nipple outward, then curved up along her rib cage. It was a scar you would never forget once you saw it, and the sight of it twisted Joey's gut.

Sure she would be upset with him if she saw him there, he reached for the door. But that's as far as he got. Suddenly she blinked open her eyes and saw him. Her hands stilled in her hair.

Any minute, he expected her to make a sudden move to shield her breast, but to his surprise she didn't. He saw no anger in her eyes, either. Maybe a twinge of uncertainty, but he could handle that. He said, "I came to wash your back, darlin'."

"Is that all you came for?"

"No. I came to say good morning."

"Would that be a long good morning? Or are you in a hurry?" She lowered her hands and stepped out of the shower spray. "Before you answer that, take a good look, Joey. If you decide you're in a hurry...I'll understand."

Chapter 8

"This is insane, Joe. The craziest idea you've ever had. You show up over two hours late for our meeting, and then you offer this as your plan."

"It'll work," Joey insisted. "It's a good plan."

"It's a piece of crap," Jackson argued. "Suicide!"

From behind his office desk, Joey glanced at Lucky, who was behind the bar sipping on a late lunch.

Lucky shrugged. "I didn't think he was going to go for it, *fratello*."

Jackson turned and scowled at Lucky. "And you do?"

"I didn't at first. There's risks involved. But the more I think on it, like Joey says, it's a good plan."

Jackson spun back around. "I won't do it!"

Joey ignored Jackson's outburst and said, "The best part is, we can move as soon as we iron out the rough spots."

Jackson snorted. "That would be the entire plan. Every part of it is rough."

"The sooner we hit Carlo, Jacky, the better."

"That's the only thing we've agreed on so far, Joe."

Joey looked to Lucky. "So what do you think? Think we can get it put together in twenty-four hours?"

Jackson swore. "Don't ask him what he thinks. That's like asking a blazing fire how hungry it is. You know he's going to want to do it just because I think it stinks."

"Where the hell are the reserves, Joey?" Lucky's voice was muffled this time. He was on his knees behind the bar looking for more scotch. "We can't be out."

"It wouldn't surprise me, the way you're always raiding my stock," Joey complained, knowing the truth of the matter was that he'd stashed the extra bottles behind the vodka. If Lucky was going to drink, he'd have to work for it. He glanced at Jackson. "What the hell are you looking at?"

"You. Your eyes are starting to look like Lucky's. You taking up drinking, or haven't you been sleeping? And just why were you two hours late? You never said. Niccolo keep you up half the night?"

"Actually, he did," Joey offered, not willing to explain what had kept him up after his son had finally fallen asleep. Or why he'd been two hours late. "So we'll put this idea on paper and see what it looks like, right?"

Jackson paced to the window. "There's got to be a better way."

"Gettin' old, or soft, Jacky?" Lucky's voice was no longer muffled. He was back on his feet, uncorking one of the elusive bottles of scotch he'd unearthed from behind the vodka.

Jackson turned, held up his middle finger and waved it at Lucky.

Joey leaned back in his desk chair and watched the show, as Lucky waved back using the same finger.

Jackson came back to the desk. If his eyes had been bullets, Lucky would have been back on his knees.

"If Jacky goes over that bar, Lucky, I'm not going to stop him," Joey warned. "Now let's get back to the plan. So you're out, then. Is that it, Jacky?"

When Jackson didn't answer, Joey said, "Fine. We'll get someone else to take your place. If you don't want to be involved, I understand. No pressure and no hard feelings."

"No hard feelings?" It was Lucky's voice. "Hell, yes, there will be hard feelings. He's the best, Joey. I won't agree to the plan if Jacky's out."

This time it was Joey's turn to swear. "I'm going

through with this plan. So decide here and now if you're players or not. If you two are so cozy that you can't be separated, then I don't need either of you. You got a minute to make up your minds."

"You can't do this alone, Joe," Jackson argued.

Lucky rounded the bar. "You called the plan crazy, Jacky. That's the beauty of it. It's so far to the left, Carlo won't see us coming. All joking aside, we can't do this without you, *fratello*."

As he passed Jackson on his way to Joey's desk, Lucky wrapped his arm around his friend's shoulder. "Come, let's sit down and talk some more. If I can strengthen that limb we're going to climb out on, maybe then you'll agree it's worth the risks."

An hour later, after Lucky had convinced Jackson to agree to the plan, Joey produced two pictures and shoved them across his desk. "Take a look at these. They were taken this morning."

Lucky picked up the pictures and shared them with Jackson. One was of a suit-and-tie bull-neck climbing into a black limo at the airport. The other was of a narrow-shouldered man with a crop of long red hair, wearing jeans and cowboy boots.

Finally, Jackson tossed the pictures back on the desk. "So Mickey Norelli and Carmine Solousi have arrived."

Joey nodded. "That means Lucky's information is right. Both men have accepted Carlo's contract."

"I met Mickey once," Jackson said. "He's a real psycho."

"Guess we'll be climbing out on that limb sooner than we thought," Lucky said. "You talk to Frank about how you want to play this?"

"That's next, right after we agree on when and where. Then I'll tell him what we've decided."

"He won't like it," Lucky warned.

Joey stood. "He doesn't have to like it—just be willing to do what I tell him."

"That'll be new for Frank—" Lucky said, "—doing what you tell him. In fact, it'll be a first."

Rhea found the passageway by accident. Or maybe not really by accident. She'd gone looking for a bottle of wine and that's when she discovered the door disguised as part of the mirrored wall behind the bar. At first she thought it was a storage room, and she was half right. The room was lined with wine racks. But beyond the racks she found another narrow passageway, and beyond that, another door.

Glad that Opal was still there to watch over Nicci, she opened the next door and stepped into another small room. Feeling as if she'd walked straight into a James Bond movie, Rhea blinked, then blinked again. The room was a wall-to-wall arsenal—every kind of gun and knife imaginable hung on the wall.

Rhea stood a moment just staring, then found the courage to move farther into the room. *I know what kind of legacy I've given my son.* As she replayed Joey's words in her mind, she became aware that the room was unusually cool. Curious as to why that was, she went deeper into the room and discovered another door. She gripped the knob, and as she drew it open, she knew immediately where the circular stairs led.

A blast of cold air swirled down the stairway to meet her as she started up. On reaching the top, she swung open another door and stepped out onto the rooftop of Masado Towers.

She glanced around, assessing the large space that had been turned into a terrace complete with sturdy tables and chairs in an ornate heavy black iron. In the summertime, she imagined, the chairs would have cushions and the massive urns that decorated the space would be full of flowers. There was even a bricked-in grill for cooking.

She didn't know how long she stood there staring, first at Joey's private outside world, as safe and well guarded as his penthouse, then at the view of the city. But suddenly she knew she wasn't alone and she whirled around to find Joey standing in the doorway watching her.

He said, "I missed having a backyard so I turned the roof into one."

He was wearing jeans and a black leather jacket. Not what he had gone to work in, which meant he'd been home for a while and had changed clothes.

"It's freezing out here, darlin'. Come on. Let's go back inside."

Hugging herself, Rhea shook her head. "I saw the

guns.'' When he said nothing, she turned back to look out over the city. ''I know what you do.''

''Do you?''

She turned back. ''I'm not stupid.''

''No, you're not.''

Rhea hugged herself tighter, the cold starting to make her teeth chatter. She knew he noticed.

He shrugged out of his leather jacket. ''You can be stubborn, you know.'' He reached around her and tucked her into his coat. Curling his fingers over the open edges, he dragged her close and kissed her hard, his mouth taking possession. Within seconds, desire settled into Rhea's limbs and she sagged against him.

It was a long time before he lifted his head, but when he did, he said, ''I'm no saint, Rhea. You knew that three years ago. But you also know that I'm not a monster.'' He placed his fingers against her lips when she attempted to speak. ''Shh... I had planned to explain some things to you tonight, but something's come up and I need to be somewhere within the hour.'' He checked his watch, then pulled her toward the open door. ''I can't be late.''

''Late for what?''

He didn't answer. Instead he said, ''I could be gone half the night. Don't wait up. I'll see you in the morning.''

At one-thirty a.m., Joey headed back to Masado Towers in his black Jaguar. Seated beside him, Frank puffed on his cigar, in a sour mood. As Lucky had predicted, it had taken over two hours that afternoon to convince their father that he needed to leave town.

Joey glanced at his father. "Lucky's arranged your route. It'll be a long trip, but in a few days you'll be back at Santa Palazzo."

"I told you before, it doesn't matter what happens to me now. What's important is the family, Rhea, Niccolo, Grace and Elena."

Joey thought he heard his father's voice falter. He glanced over and said, "This is going to work, Frank. It's a good plan."

"Have you forgiven me?"

"Let's not go there."

"I don't deserve it, Joey, but I—"

"Twenty-four years ago, you did what you thought you had to, Frank. Three years ago, you again thought you were justified. Let's let it go at that."

"When you two boys were knee-high, I should have whipped your butts for calling me Frank. I should have made you call me *padre,* or dad. I always wanted to hear you call me something other than Frank."

The confession hung in the silence.

"Are you sure there isn't a way to send Rhea and Niccolo with me?"

Joey shook his head. "That's not how the plan works. For everything to fit, they need to stay behind. At least for now. That's the only part of this I don't like, but if we can get Carlo to play the game our way, then we have a chance to take him down."

Joey took a left off of Michigan Avenue and headed for the parking garage beneath Masado Towers. As he passed through the gates, he nodded to the night watchman, then found his reserved parking space not far from the elevators.

"You packed earlier, right?"

"Yes. Lucky already picked up my bags. I admit I'm anxious to see Grace. About Elena…"

Joey checked his watch. "You don't have to explain, Frank. I'm a father myself, and no one needs to tell me how that feels. Let's go."

It was as they climbed out of the black Jaguar and started for the elevator that Joey heard the sound of squealing tires. He spun around just as a blue van, a Masado company van, came into sight, racing along the narrow aisles like a demon from hell. The van bore down on them, its speed increasing. Suddenly it swerved sideways, and Joey saw an AR-18 poke out of the open window.

He yelled at Frank to get down, just as an explosion of gunfire echoed through the underground garage. He heard his father cry out, watched him jerk hard to the left. Saw blood spread across Frank's chest.

It all happened so fast that by the time Joey reached for his 9-mm Beretta, three more shots were fired. He felt pain explode in his right shoulder, but managed to get off two shots before he dropped to his knees. Glancing quickly at his shoulder, he saw that he was leaking blood as rapidly as Frank. He crawled to where his father lay on the concrete. He heard the van squeal to a stop. Heard a door slam. He got to his feet, grabbed Frank under the arms and dragged him behind the Jag.

More shots were fired, only this time they came from somewhere behind him. Joey spun around, aimed his Beretta, then relaxed his hand when he saw two of his men running toward them.

A car door slammed again, then he heard the van peel out. Joey looked down at his father covered in blood. Heart racing, he searched for a pulse. Behind him, he heard one of the guards screaming for an ambulance, screaming that the boss was dead. "*Maledizione*, they whacked him! They cut Frank down on his own turf!"

As the man skidded to a stop in front of the Jag, Joey pulled Frank onto his side and shouted, "Stay back! Get the hell back!" Then, as he hovered over his father to shield him, he reached into his pocket and pulled out his cell phone. After he punched in Lucky's number and heard his brother's voice, he said, "Frank's…dead. I'm hit."

As Joey disconnected, he continued to protect his father from the growing crowd that gathered. With a shaky hand, he reached out and touched the black eye patch that covered his father's right eye. Finally, he whispered, "It wasn't supposed to be like this. You bleeding in the street. I'm sorry…*mio padre*."

* * *

It was five in the morning before Joey, accompanied by Jackson, was allowed to leave Memorial Hospital. He was in a great deal of pain due to the bullet that had passed through his shoulder, but that wasn't where his thoughts were. They were on his father and the Masado blood that had been spilled hours ago because of Carlo Talupa.

"Hank Mallory will do what he can, Joe," Jackson assured. "He'll run interference with the news media for as long as he can, but you know as well as I do that this is big news. By noon, everyone in Chicago will be reading about how Frank Masado was taken out while his son and guards stood by and watched. How's the shoulder?"

"It's fine."

"Like hell it is. I know what it feels like getting pierced. Need some painkillers?"

"No."

"Where did Lucky take off to?" Jackson asked as they crossed the street and headed for the hospital parking lot.

"He went to the morgue. I wanted him to wait so I could go with him, but he said he wanted to go alone. He blames himself for things going sour. But it's my fault, not his. It was my plan."

"It's over, Joe. We all knew the risks. If Frank was standing here, he wouldn't be pointing a finger at anyone."

Joey glanced down at the sling that drew his arm

close to his body, then up at the falling snow. When they reached the car, Jackson swiped the snow off the hood, then leaned his backside against it and shoved his hands in his jeans pockets. Joey took a position beside him. Minutes later, he winced, then swore, as he attempted to reach inside his pocket and pull out his cigarettes.

Jackson said, "Here, let me help." As he dug into Joey's coat to retrieve the cigarettes, he said, "This might be a good time to think about quitting this nasty habit."

"Just because you quit cold turkey doesn't mean I can."

Jackson poked the cigarette between Joey's lips, then fired it up. "I'm sorry Frank was shot."

Joey pulled the cigarette from his mouth and blew smoke. "You warned me the plan stunk."

"No, you were right. It was a good plan. It was just risky as hell. Come on. Let me take you home."

Joey dug in his pocket and came up with his keys. "I've driven before one-armed. You go home to Sunni. I can manage."

Jackson stripped the keys from Joey's hand. "I know you *can* get yourself home, but you don't need to since I'm here."

Without further argument, Joey climbed into the passenger side and leaned his head back against the seat. His shoulder throbbed and he closed his eyes as Jackson slid behind the wheel. A few minutes

later, as they started back to Masado Towers, he said,
"I need to make the funeral arrangements."

"I can help with that."

"I've been thinking about a few other things. After the way this turned out tonight, I need to make sure that Niccolo and Rhea are taken care of in case I'm—"

Jackson turned over the engine. "Nothing more is going to go wrong, Joe. We're going to get Carlo. After tonight, we'll concentrate on going after Solousi. We'll tighten the noose, and when he makes his move—"

"That move will be at the funeral."

"You think so?" Jackson pulled out of the parking lot, then headed back to Masado Towers.

"I do. Carlo will see it as the perfect time and place to show the *famiglia* how powerful he is and that he's still the bossman in Chicago. And whatever happens, I need to make sure my son's future is secure and that Rhea will be taken care of."

"Hell, Joe, I don't want to hear this."

"If you were in my shoes and I was in yours, Jacky, I imagine you'd be thinking similar thoughts. And whether I liked hearing what you had to say or not, I'd listen. Then I would do whatever it was you asked of me."

Forty minutes later, Joey walked into the penthouse to find Rhea pacing like a caged animal. It was obvious she had already heard the news. Her face was tear-stained and her eyes were red and full of fear.

He saw her eyes lock on his arm in the sling. Saw her shudder.

"Oh God, it's true! Opal called and said that Frank…that he…that he was killed tonight and that you'd been shot."

The sudden flood of tears and the devastation in her voice knifed Joey in the gut. He carefully shrugged his jacket off his shoulders and dropped it on the sofa. "I wanted to be the one to tell you. To explain how—"

"How you got Frank killed?"

Joey blinked, saw her fear turn into anger. "Listen, Rhea. If you'll just sit down, I'll explain how—"

"I don't want to sit down, Joey. And I don't want to hear your excuses. How one of your *assistants* slipped up. Or how it wasn't supposed to happen this way. I know firsthand how lacking your security is. How easy it is to trick your men. Obviously, Carlo Talupa knew it, too."

Her words were as cold as the icy chip she now wore on her shoulder. Joey stepped forward and reached out to her with his healthy arm, but she backed up.

"I should have demanded that you send us back that first day. I knew something like this could happen. Knew all of it."

"Then, maybe you should have told me *all of it* the minute you arrived."

Her chin quivered. "Why didn't you just face me at Santa Palazzo? If you had, none of this would have happened."

"Maybe we should back it up farther than that. Maybe if I hadn't gotten you pregnant. Or maybe if you hadn't run from me once you found out. Or maybe if I hadn't given you a ride home from the hospital that first night I saw you. Okay, darlin', I'm to blame! I screwed up, and because of it, Frank's dead!"

Joey hadn't meant to shout. He hadn't meant to lose control.

She turned away. It was as if the sight of him suddenly turned her stomach.

"I can't believe he's gone. Poor Grace. And... Elena. Oh God, what will I tell them? In Grace's condition, how will I be able to make her understand that she'll never see Frank again?"

"You don't have to tell her, Rhea. It's already been taken care of."

She spun toward him. "You called Santa Palazzo? Told them Frank's dead? Are you crazy? Grace is ill. Elena has no idea that you and Lucky even exist. Oh God, I have to go to them. I have to—"

Joey reached out and grabbed her arm as she attempted to hurry past him. "No! Not now."

"You can't stop me." She wrenched her arm from him, and in doing so, jarred his shoulder.

He swore, then stepped back. "I can stop you, Rhea, and I will. It's not safe for you to go anywhere near Santa Palazzo. It's not safe for you and Niccolo, or Grace and Elena. And it won't be, until I've got Carlo hanging by his heels.''

''I don't give a damn about Carlo Talupa!'' Tears clung to her cheeks and shimmered in her eyes. ''How can you be so unfeeling? Frank's dead! Or doesn't that matter to you? I can see that it doesn't. You never understood him. Never knew the real Frank. Not Frank Palazzo.''

This time it was Joey's turn to walk away. He headed for the bar, his guts were in a knot and his head was pounding. He wrenched a bottle of scotch off the shelf, then headed toward his bedroom. ''I'm through fighting with you, Rhea. There's a lot I have to see to in the next few days. Arrangements that need to be made.''

''I want to leave here, Joey. I want to take Nicci and leave Chicago.''

He stopped, turned. ''No.''

''Damn you, Joey.''

''And damn you right back, Rhea. I may not have your respect at the moment, but I'll have your loyalty. You're stuck between a hard place and an even harder man, darlin'. But it's not news who and what I am. The sooner you get used to that, the better off you're going to be. Whether you like it or not, you are here and you are mine. That is your future, and my son's.''

She shook her head, her eyes wide. ''What are you saying?''

"I'm saying, in three days I'm going to bury my father in Rosewood Cemetery. I'm saying, you're going to be there standing right beside me…as my wife. No one will deny my son what is rightfully his. Not Carlo Talupa and not you. Niccolo will have my name. *Capiche?*"

"You can't be serious. Carlo Talupa just killed your father, and now you intend to mock him by marrying me? No! You can't. I won't do it!"

"I'd tell you to trust me on this, but it's clear you're not thinking straight right now, so I'll save my breath. Our wedding will be here, the day after tomorrow. Jacky and Lucky are seeing to the details."

She continued to shake her head, her sapphire-blue eyes as big as he'd ever seen them.

"I won't do it, Joey. You can't force me."

"If I have to drag you kicking and screaming, I will, Rhea. But I don't think that's going to be necessary. You'll agree to become my wife because the one thing I'm sure of is that you love my son and you're an excellent *madre*. A mother who will do anything to save her son's life and secure his future. Even if it means marrying the man she hates right now."

Chapter 9

What saved Rhea from turning into an emotional wreck over the next two days was seeing to Nicci's needs and remembering Frank with fond memories. Like the look on his face at the hospital in Key West when he'd first arrived carrying two dozen red roses and a teddy bear wearing an eye patch.

In that moment she had known why Grace had fallen in love with Frank Masado. And she had come to understand the depth of his goodness underneath his hard-as-iron image.

You're stuck between a hard place and an even harder man, darlin'.

Joey's words still plagued her. They hadn't spoken since she had accused him of killing his father. She was sorry for that. Joey hadn't killed Frank. She'd just felt so much guilt that she'd lashed out at the one person she knew was strong enough to take it.

But she'd been wrong to do it, and since then Joey had been spending most of his time somewhere else. That somewhere, she'd learned last night, was the Stardust.

"Nana said Daddy's still seeping, Mama."

Rhea blinked out of her reverie and saw her son heading for his father's bedroom. Before she could stop Nicci from bursting in on Joey, the door was open and he'd disappeared inside.

"Nicci…"

Rhea entered Joey's bedroom to find Nicci already making his way up the stairs.

"Nicci…"

Ignoring her, he wiggled himself onto the bed before Rhea reached the second level. As she followed, intending to scoop him up, she was momentarily distracted by the two empty liquor bottles on the nightstand.

From the nightstand, her gaze traveled to the bed where Nicci had fit himself close to his father. Joey's chest was bare and his head rested on a red satin pillow. His tousled hair made him look younger, his worries eased in sleep. He wasn't wearing the sling. Instead, a large white bandage covered his right shoulder.

Guilt overwhelmed Rhea, and shame followed. She'd been devastated to hear about Frank, but she had also been horrified by the fact that Joey had been almost killed, too. That Carlo Talupa was still out there, and that at any moment Joey could be taken from her.

And it was all her fault. By allowing Sophia D'Lano to see her and Nicci that first night at the Stardust, she'd turned a dangerous situation into a disaster. If she hadn't gone looking for Joey that night, Frank might still be alive.

"Mama," Nicci whispered. "What's dat?"

Rhea had been studying Joey's muscular chest and the low-riding sheet that revealed one very naked thigh. She now saw that her son was pointing to the bandage. "Daddy had an accident, Nicci."

"Did he cwy?"

The question gave Rhea pause. "I don't think so, sweetie."

Nicci suddenly reached to touch the injury. In re-action, Rhea's hand shot out and grabbed his wrist. "No, Nicci. Don't touch it."

When she let go of his wrist, Nicci lowered his head. "I sorry, Mama. I no hurt Daddy. I pomis."

"You can touch me, *figlio*. You won't hurt me."

Rhea started, then looked over to see Joey's eyes sharper than she had imagined they would be, con-sidering all the scotch he had obviously consumed the night before.

"What time is it?" he asked.

"Nine-thirty."

He moaned as he rolled onto his good shoulder, then shoved himself up.

Immediately, Nicci saw an opportunity to come to his father's aid, and he stacked the pillows behind Joey to make him more comfortable. "Nana's made juice. Want some, Daddy?"

"Sounds good."

"I get it." Nicci looked at Rhea. "Otay, Mama?"

"If you walk slow and tell Nana not to fill the glass full."

On a mission, Nicci slid off the bed, and was halfway across the room by the time Rhea started after him.

"Can you toss my robe up here before he comes back, Rhea?"

She turned back to see him pointing to the dark red robe draped over the couch. She retrieved it, then started back to the bed, as Joey sat up and dropped his feet onto the floor. Slowly he rolled his injured shoulder.

"Is it serious?"

He looked up. "No. The bullet went in and out."

She was aware that the red sheet was doing a poor job of covering him, aware that he was semi-aroused. Closing in on the bed, she said, "Don't you think you should be wearing the sling?"

"It's not comfortable."

"It's not supposed to be comfortable, it's supposed to protect your shoulder while it heals."

"Help me get the robe on, would you? Before Niccolo comes back."

Rhea realized that Joey viewed his situation as a

weakness. And, of course, it would never do for a Masado to be seen as vulnerable and weak, especially in front of his son. He stood slowly. Naked, he held up his good arm and she slipped the robe around him, then worked carefully to get his injured arm into the other sleeve.

One quick glance told her that the robe would do him little good as it was, and that prompted her to reach for the dangling ends of the belt. But by the time she'd secured the robe at his waist, his problem had doubled.

"What else can I do?" she asked softly, and the question hung between them, as heavy as Joey's arousal.

Finally, he said, "Stop blaming yourself for what happened."

Rhea gave in to the moment. "I was wrong to accuse you of killing Frank. I didn't mean that."

"I know. You blame yourself. And that's crazy."

"It's not crazy. We both know that if Sophia hadn't seen me that first night at the Stardust, none of this would be happening."

"We don't know that, Rhea."

"I know it, Joey." She touched his face, then turned and started down the steps. Over her shoulder, she said, "I pray that Grace and Elena will someday forgive me. But I won't blame them if they can't because I will never forgive myself."

"Daddy!"

Rhea was getting accustomed to the lopsided grin

Nicci wore whenever his father was around. Looking up from where she sat on the sofa, she saw Joey enter the living room. His feet were bare and his mood was hidden behind heavy-lidded eyes and two days' growth of whiskers. He was wearing jeans and a white shirt that he hadn't bothered to button—or maybe he hadn't been able to button it.

The silver cross around his neck gave her pause, and she realized that he must have found it where she'd left it in his room. The night she found the passageway—the night Frank had been killed—she had remembered that she hadn't given it back to him, and she'd retrieved it from her things and had left it on his nightstand.

Nicci wiggled off the sofa and, as he reached Joey, grabbed his father's legs and clung to him. As naturally as if he'd been doing it for years, Joey bent and scooped up his son with his good arm.

Rhea saw him wince and said, "I don't think carrying him is going to do your arm any good."

"Maybe not." He pulled Nicci close and rubbed his unshaven jaw gently over his son's cheek. "But I like holding him. Pretty soon he'll be too big." He winked at Nicci and his son's grin widened. "So what have you and Mama been doing today?"

Nicci pointed to the book that Rhea held. "I got a new book from Nana. A daa-gon book. Wanna see?"

Joey carried Nicci to where Rhea sat and eased down beside her. Nicci promptly settled himself half on Joey's leg and half on Rhea's. Then he laid the book open on his lap and pointed to the purple dragon breathing fire. "Jus like Purple Pete, Daddy. He looks mean, but he yikes kids. Jus like Papa Fank yikes me."

His innocent words were followed by silence. Rhea refused to look at Joey, and she was hoping he wouldn't say anything about Frank to their son. She wasn't sure how to tell Nicci that his Papa was gone, so she had decided to forgo it for now.

As Nicci paged through the book, he talked to Joey nonstop, pointing to the dragon each time it appeared, which was every page. Twice Rhea looked up to find Joey watching her over his son's head, and both times she quickly looked away.

The heat generated between their bodies added to the awkwardness as the minutes slowly ticked by. The afternoon was nearly gone, and by seven she would be Mrs. Joey Masado.

The irony was that for three years she'd day-dreamed about marrying Joey. She'd spent hours on the beach at Santa Palazzo imagining how he would sweep her into his arms and claim that he had never stopped looking for her. Then he would tell her he loved her, something he had never said. And he would speak the words in Italian. He would say, "*Ti amo,* darlin'. Forever, *Ti amo.*"

"Rhea, did you hear me?"

She started. "What?"

"I said Lavina Ward will be coming to the wedding. She's insisted that she bring the wedding cake. And Jacky's going to bring Sunni to be your maid of honor.''

Opal entered the living room looking at her watch. ''I believe Nicci's overdue for a nap.''

Rhea glanced down to see that her son was fighting to keep his eyes open. She reached down and closed the book. Then Opal stepped forward and took Nicci into her arms.

''Come on, little one. Time for the sandman to pay you a visit.''

After Opal headed down the hall with Nicci's head on her shoulder, Rhea found herself the center of Joey's interest. He didn't say anything, just stared at her until she began to feel self-conscious. She started to get up, but he put his hand on her thigh. Squeezing gently, he said, ''I have something for you.''

He raised his sore arm and slowly dug into his shirt pocket and produced a sparkling diamond ring. Rhea stared at it as he clasped her hand and slid the ring onto her finger.

A symbol of love was the accepted meaning behind such an expensive and beautiful gift. But Joey spoke no words of love, made no promises—just looked at his watch and said, ''I've got some things to attend to, and I'm supposed to meet Jacky and Lucky in my office to go over a few details for tomorrow's funeral. I'll see you at seven.''

The outside door closed moments later, and Rhea lowered her eyes to the flashy diamond on her finger.

Left to contemplate the future, she couldn't help wondering what Frank would have said. Would he agree with Joey, that marrying her was the answer? Or would he think it was a mistake?

A mistake that could get Joey killed.

Sunni Blais brought roses. Jackson brought Mac, his retired German shepherd partner, to meet Nicci. Lucky came with the priest, and Lavina Ward arrived carrying a three-layered white cake with a small plastic bride and groom sitting on top.

At exactly seven o'clock, dressed in a black dress with a high collar and long fitted sleeves, Rhea entered the living room. She had decided that the powder-blue jersey dress and satin shoes she'd found in the gold boxes on her bed an hour ago were inappropriate, and the situation being what it was, a black dress made more sense.

She noted that Sunni Blais wore a rose-colored silk suit, and Jackson and Lucky were dressed in formal black. Rhea couldn't help but think they would be wearing those same suits tomorrow, and that thought sent raw chills up her spine. She struggled fiercely to contain unwelcome tears.

The large living room was full of bloodred roses, and she realized that the money spent to make a statement in a room this size must have been considerable.

A glance around the room located Nicci sitting on the floor beside Mac. Her son wore black dress pants

similar to those of the other men, black shoes, and a
white shirt with a black vest and red bow tie. Surprised, she realized that Joey must have shopped for
both of them. Or maybe it had been Jean, his secretary.

Joey stood in front of the window talking to
Lucky. He was outfitted in black, as well, one hand
in his pocket, his head lowered as he listened to
Lucky, who had a glass of scotch in his hand.

It was obvious Joey and his brother were discussing something other than the wedding. Lucky seemed
to go on and on, and yet Joey never looked away. It
appeared the Masado boys worked day and night,
something they had been taught over the years by
example. Frank's example.

Frank. Rhea wasn't sure she was going to be able
to get through tomorrow. She'd lost one father already, and even though she'd been very young and
she hadn't known her father all that well, the memory
still devastated her.

What would it be like to say goodbye to a man
who had truly become a caring father to her in every
sense of the word? The father she had always longed
for. A father who had sacrificed so much to keep the
people he loved safe. A father who had valued her
enough to protect her with his life, and to offer her
a place in his family.

She had never seen Frank Masado until he'd
knocked on her door that cold November day three
years ago. But just as Joey had rescued her that night

at the hospital so long ago, Frank had come to rescue her, too. Even though, at the time, she had no idea she needed rescuing.

But he had known, and like a fierce lion protecting his pride, he'd swept her out of danger and saved her and his unborn grandson.

"Rhea, I'm Sunni."

Rhea blinked and focused on Jackson's fiancée, the lovely black-haired Sunni Blais. Her hair was swept up into a messy knot, and she was everything Rhea had ever wanted to be—successful and gorgeous. Flawless.

Rhea held out her hand. "I'm glad to meet you. You have a beautiful shop. I spent some time at Silks the other day."

Sunni took Rhea's hand and squeezed it gently. "I've been wanting to meet you, the love of Joey's life."

The comment surprised Rhea. Obviously Sunni thought that because Joey was marrying her, he loved her. She didn't bother to dispute the perfect illusion. Instead, she said, "I hear you'll be getting married soon yourself."

Sunni glanced over her shoulder at Jackson. "Yes, I am. I still can't believe Jack wants to marry me. But we never know, do we—" she turned back "—why the men we love, love us back. For years I hid behind my diabetes, afraid to trust a man with my heart. Then along comes Jack, bold and wonderful, in-your-face Jackson Ward, claiming to be *the man*. He's the man, all right.'' Her gaze drifted to Nicci. ''You're very lucky, you know. I would love to give Jack a child, but my doctor doesn't advise it.''

Rhea felt instantly ashamed. She knew better than to make quick judgments of people, and yet she had done so the moment she laid eyes on Sunni. The truth was, everyone lived with flaws and disappointments. Some were visible, and others lay tucked away where no one could see them. ''He's absolutely adorable,'' Sunni was saying. ''Nicci is a miniature of Joey.''

The comment sent Rhea's attention to her son, who lay on his belly examining Mac's huge feet while the dog licked her son's face.

''I hope you don't mind that we brought Mac along. Jack lectured him on the way over, so I'm sure he understands how important it is to be on his best behavior tonight.''

''I warned him there would be no TV for a week if he screws up.'' The words were Jackson's as he joined them and slipped his arm around Sunni. ''You look pretty, Rhea.''

''I look like I'm in mourning, Jackson. And I am,'' she said, realizing only after she'd said the words that they sounded hostile and bitter.

''Joey said you were taking this hard.''

''Frank made a lifetime mistake that haunted him for years. But he tried to make up for it the best way he could.''

''Yes, he did,'' Jackson agreed.

"Then, how fair is it that in the end he lost the fight? A fight he deserved to win."

"Life isn't always fair, Rhea. You know that. But, yes, Frank deserved to get out alive."

Rhea glanced away, fighting tears. When her eyes met Joey's hard gaze, she realized he was studying her dress. Suddenly he left Lucky and started across the room toward her, rounding Sunni and Jackson to stand beside her.

Taking her hand, he said to Jackson, "Will you excuse us for a few minutes?" Then he led her down the hall and into her bedroom.

Inside, she thought he would let her go, but instead he turned quickly and pinned her against the door. "Tell me it didn't fit."

Rhea lifted her chin. "Okay, it didn't fit...my mood."

His jaw jerked. Then he said, "My house. My rules."

"If you want me standing beside you, then you'll have to make an exception this time, Joey."

"Don't be stubborn today, Rhea. I want you to wear the blue dress and shoes." He reached up and brushed his fingers over her lips, then slid his hand around her neck, his fingers sliding into her hair. "Please..."

He was such a powerful man, so very handsome, and, yes, his deep voice and his satin-smooth touch could seduce a saint.

Determined, she said, "I prefer black today."

"And I prefer you looking like a bride today."

"I'm not going to change." Rhea's heart started to pound.

He noticed and he leaned forward and ran his tongue over her lower lip. "Why fight me, when you know I'm going to win, anyway?" That said, he slid his hands along her rib cage, his thumbs going wide to catch her breasts. Then slowly, he leaned in and kissed her, coaxing her into giving back.

Rhea wanted to resist, but it was impossible when he was this close. He hadn't kissed her in three days, and she had no strength left. She opened her mouth, let him in—

"Joey, the priest is starting to pace and look at his watch." It was Lucky's voice outside the door.

Joey stepped back and said, "We'll be right there. Come on, I'll help you change."

When he released her, Rhea watched him head for the bed to retrieve the dress, and when he was far enough away for her to escape, she simply slipped out the door.

Back in the living room, she was suddenly confronted by Lavina Ward, who came rushing forward. With a look of concern on her face, Jackson's mother said, "Something old, something new, something borrowed, something blue. Do you have it all, dear?"

It was then that Rhea realized why Joey had bought the blue shimmering jersey dress and the new shoes. She glanced at him as he appeared in the hall. The priest cleared his throat, and she glanced over to see he was drumming his fingers on the edge of the bar.

She offered him a placating smile, then said, "I'll be right back. I need five more minutes."

The wedding lasted twelve minutes. Dressed in blue and wearing Joey's cross around her neck—something borrowed—Rhea became Mrs. Joey Masado at seven forty-five on November eleventh.

As much as the priest appeared to be in a rush, Lavina Ward convinced him to stay for a piece of cake, and he was still there an hour later when Rhea spied Joey talking to him, their son asleep on his father's injured shoulder.

"I'll put him to bed," she said softly when she approached the two men. Joey didn't argue as he slowly slid Nicci off his shoulder.

Inside the bedroom, Rhea dressed her sleepy son for bed. She was tucking him in with his teddy bear beside him when she heard the door open behind her. She turned to see Lucky standing in the doorway. Straightening, unsure what to say, she whispered, "I'm sorry about Frank."

"It's not your fault, Rhea." He stepped into the room and closed the door. Like Joey, Lucky looked very handsome in his black suit—handsome in a wild, hell-raising sort of way.

His nickname fit him perfectly, and there was no mystery as to how he'd earned the name once you started to count the visible scars. He had one on his hand, and there was a vivid inch-long mark on his chin. The one that ran down the side of his neck was half hidden by the length of his hair, and it was only when he turned his head a certain way that you could see that the scar started somewhere behind his ear and disappeared into his shirt collar.

She had noticed that he'd been drinking scotch all night, and he still was.

He came toward the bed and surprised her by reaching down and running his hand gently over his nephew's silky black hair. Nicci was asleep and he didn't move, just snuggled deeper into the warm blankets next to his bear.

"Joey got a call and he had to take off. Some business that couldn't wait. He wanted me to tell you he would be late."

"Business? Tonight?"

He stepped back and shoved his hand into his pocket. "Don't worry about *mio fratello*. I won't let anything happen to him."

"Can you guarantee that, Lucky?"

"Right now, Jacky's with him. And I will join both of them soon. This business tonight isn't dangerous. Just necessary."

"Your father told me once that Carlo Talupa was unstoppable. Tell me that's not true."

"When Joey wants something, he's the one who is unstoppable."

"And what does Joey want, Lucky?"

"That's a question with many answers. I think it would be best if you ask your husband that, not me."

Rhea nodded.

He stepped forward and suddenly brushed a warm kiss to her right cheek, then one to the left. "Welcome to the family, *bello*. You are good for Joey. I have always known it. Because you are, know that my commitment to him and my nephew is strong, and that it is just as strong to you. These are hard times, but we are hard men. Frank taught *mio fratello* and me to be survivors, and so we are. Things will get better soon. Trust that, and your husband."

Joey found Rhea asleep on his bed when he returned to the penthouse at two in the morning. She was still wearing the blue dress he'd bought her for their wedding, and there was an empty wine bottle on the table as well as an empty glass.

He frowned, not comfortable with her drinking. It made him question why she had felt the need, and he didn't like what he came up with for an answer.

She had an enormous amount of guilt over Frank, and he wanted to ease that guilt.

He removed his suit jacket, then crossed the room and mounted the steps. She was so damn beautiful...beautiful and his wife.

Mio moglie.

The words made lust coil deep in Joey's gut, and a heavy ache settle between his legs. Needing to touch her, he brushed his hand over her breasts, then down her flat stomach. One knee braced on the bed, he bent down to kiss her. Needing more, his hand slid over her hip and slowly he pulled the dress up to reveal her beautiful legs.

He kissed her delicate knees, then slid his hand beneath the dress to stroke her thighs. He heard her sigh, and he curved his hand over the top of her thigh and slid it between her legs. Another sigh and she relaxed her knees.

Joey backed away and removed her shoes, and then his hands were pushing the dress higher to remove her panties. He slid them off her hips, over her thighs and past her knees. Gently, rolling her side to side to free them from her body, he moaned when the white satin thong settled in his hand.

"Joey…"

"I'm here." He brought his head up to see that her sleepy eyes were open and her lips were parted.

"I was afraid you wouldn't come back."

"Is that why you were drinking?"

For several seconds she didn't say anything, then she sat up and slid forward. As she did, it sent the slippery jersey higher, offering Joey a glimpse of her silky blond triangle.

He moaned, then crouched in front of her, shoved the dress to her waist. Leaning forward, he kissed her gently, whispered, "I want to taste you."

He felt her shiver at his suggestion, then her hands began to work open the buttons on his shirt. After she'd peeled it off him, she leaned forward and kissed the white bandage covering his shoulder.

Quietly, against his neck, she said, "Help me, Joey. Help me forget what will come with the dawn."

He stood and quickly undressed her, leaving her in only her bra. She hesitated a second, then, keeping her eyes locked with his, she reached around and unhooked the white satin. When her breasts spilled forward, he settled his gaze on her sweet flesh. Her nipples puckered for him.

"You're so beautiful, darlin'."

"You don't have to say that, Joey. I know I'm not."

"You are, darlin'. And best of all, you're mine. My wife." He leaned forward and kissed her marred breast, laid his mouth to the scar and traced it with hot kisses. When his lips curled around her nipple, she arched for him, and he suckled her, then laved and stroked.

He could feel her body trembling as he laid her back on the bed, then shed his clothes.

"All night, Joey," she whispered.

Determined to give her whatever it was she needed, Joey joined her on the bed. Her lips were parted and moist, her breathing elevated. He kissed her hungry little mouth and when she moaned, he dipped his head and kissed her belly, then moved lower. Brushing featherlight kisses over her thighs, he worked his way toward the silky curls between her legs.

She opened to him, and he slid his fingers inside her, moving them in and out. In and out. Then he brought his mouth over her and his tongue hard against her most sensitive spot.

She cried out, and as she gave herself over to him, he made sweet love to her with his tongue...then with his body, until dawn.

Chapter 10

The church was packed. Every store owner and neighbor Frank Masado had ever had dealings with, and every player in the Chicago *famiglia*, showed up to pay their respects.

Or maybe it was out of curiosity. Frank Masado had been whacked in the parking garage on his home turf. The word *whacked* stuck in Rhea's mind; she had heard it mumbled as she walked up the aisle on Joey's arm.

The service was long, as dictated by Sicilian custom. She had wanted to wear dark glasses, but Joey had refused to let her, and she had cried openly throughout the service.

As they left the church, the snow they had woken up to continued to fall, and the silvery flakes glistened on the pavement as Joey directed Rhea to the long black limousine.

He motioned to Gates, handed Nicci to him, then kissed Rhea's cheek. ''Go with Gates,'' he instructed. ''I'll meet you at Rosewood.''

''All right.''

They made eye contact, and just before he stepped away, he brushed a tear off Rhea's cheek, then kissed her lips.

The cavalcade to Rosewood Cemetery would be long. A mile-long line of black stretches waited to follow the procession.

Rhea climbed into the limousine and she snuggled into her black sable coat, a coat Joey had brought to her just after breakfast, then she removed Nicci's hat and gloves and unbuttoned his new gray coat so he wouldn't get too warm. Glancing out the window, she noticed Lavina Ward had stopped Joey. As she kissed his cheek, he spoke a few words, then looked back at the limousine where she and Nicci sat.

A few minutes later, Lavina nudged through the crowd and headed for the limo, while Joey, accompanied by Lucky, disappeared into the hearse to ride with the casket.

Norman Gates opened the door for Lavina, and after she had climbed into the limousine, he followed, taking a seat next to her, across from Rhea.

Lavina reached out and patted Rhea's hand. ''You're doing fine, dear. Here, let me take Niccolo.'' As she reached for him, she said, ''Our boy here looks exactly like Joey did at this age. I can't get over it. When I see him it just brings back so many memories. Did Joey tell you, he practically lived at my house when he was growing up? He and Jackson were inseparable when they were boys. Of course, Lucky tagged along. Then when he got a little older, the boys were tagging after him, trying to keep him out of trouble."

Lavina laughed over that, then began to tell Nicci a funny story about his father and his uncle Lucky. Rhea listened, and she thought, though Norman kept his eyes directed out the window, he was listening, too.

The trip to Rosewood took close to an hour. Once they drove through the gates, Norman said, "Mr. Masado wants you to stay in the car until he comes to get you. I'll be outside if you need anything."

When he stepped from the car and closed the door, Rhea said, "Carlo Talupa was at the church. Do you think he will be here, too?"

"Yes." Lavina slipped Nicci's hat back on his head. "He came to gloat, and to show how untouchable he is." Once again, Lavina patted Rhea's knee. "But he's gone too far this time."

Rhea frowned. "What do you mean?"

"I mean, my boys are smart, and they do not let injustice go unpunished. I'm getting old, but that doesn't mean I have an excuse to be stupid. I keep my ears open at the restaurant. Mark my words, there is a shake-up brewing." She glanced out the window.

"It looks like they will be coming to get us soon." She took Nicci's mittens from Rhea and began to slip them on his hands. "Did you know that Joey has always liked children?"

Glad for the subject change, Rhea said, "No. But he's a natural with Nicci."

"In the old neighborhood he was the one who kept watch over the forgotten ones."

"Forgotten ones?"

"That's what we called the children in the neighborhood who didn't have responsible parents for whatever reason. Frank was gone a lot, and I worked, too. Harold—that was my husband—he had diabetes and required a lot of attention. Jackson had to grow up fast on account of that. With Joey and Lucky in and out of the house so much, they helped out with Harold. I guess my boys got used to responsibility early. Maybe that's why Joey became so serious. 'A boy with an old man's soul,' is what I used to call him. To this day he's never forgotten the forgotten ones."

"What do you mean?"

"Joey is the one who started the safe house in the old neighborhood. Jackson tells me Joey is the reason the place continues to stay open twenty-four hours a day, seven days a week."

Rhea didn't know what to say. She had always known there was more to Joey than good looks and Masado Towers. Still, she had to admit she hadn't expected to hear that he funded a safe house for forgotten children.

"I can read your thoughts, dear. The Masado boys were born into the *famiglia,* just like Nicci." Lavina handed him back to Rhea. "They were born innocent boys who just wanted to play and have fun like all children do. But children grow up, and Joey and Lucky became men with heavy burdens and no way out. So they did what Frank taught them to do. They became survivors, and they learned how to change what they could change, and to live within the boundaries of what they could not. They are the crème de la crème, my boys. Our city's finest, Rhea. And don't let anyone tell you different."

A solid rap on the window warned them that things were about to change. The door opened seconds later, and Lucky dipped his head inside. To Rhea, he said, "Joey's on his way. Stay put." Then his eyes connected with Lavina's. "Come on, Vina. Jacky wants you where he can keep an eye on you."

Lavina hiked one graying eyebrow. "He does, does he?"

"Come, *Madre.*"

When he stood, Rhea spied a gun inside Lucky's jacket. She shivered at the sight, then clutched Nicci closer. Another five minutes passed before the door opened again. But Joey didn't call her out; instead, he climbed in and sat across from her.

He was dressed in a long black wool coat that made him look as dark and dangerous as Lucky. But the moment he saw Nicci, he smiled, and his son quickly wiggled off her lap to crawl up and hug his father. Remembering what Lavina had told her minutes ago, Rhea now understood why Joey and Nicci had become so inseparable—Nicci not only sensed that his father loved him, he also *liked* him. Joey's sincerity was as potent as his dark eyes and as convincing as his gentle touch.

"Once we're outside, I want you to stay close," he instructed. "Gates will be in charge of Niccolo and he will be on your left."

Rhea scowled. "Is something supposed to happen here?"

He hesitated a moment, then nodded.

"Don't you think I should know what that 'something' is, so I'll be prepared?"

"I don't want you anticipating anything. I don't want you acting nervous."

"I'm already nervous."

"All right. Jacky, along with the feds, plan to arrest Carlo Talupa after the committal. They claim they have a bookie in Allenwood willing to turn over some hard evidence. I don't think it's going to be enough to hold Carlo for long, but it'll stir things up. Right now, that works for us. It should be a clean arrest, but in case it isn't, I want you to keep your wits about you and do whatever you're told. *Capiche?*"

So that was why so many guards had been trailing them all day. At the church, it had looked like an army. Feeling another dose of fear slide up her spine,

Rhea lowered her head to hide the worry in her eyes. She knew Joey was doing what he could, but would it be enough? Could he win? Frank had told her that Carlo Talupa was unstoppable.

When Joey wants something, he's the one who is unstoppable. Lucky's words came to Rhea on a cloud of hope, and she decided she would cling to them.

"Rhea, look at me."

She took a breath, bolstered her courage, then raised her head.

"This will be over soon."

"I'll do what I'm told."

He smiled. *"Grazie."*

The word was spoken softly, and it hung between them while they stared into each other's eyes. It was a long time before she said, "We're survivors…you and I."

"*Si.* And our son will be one, too." He reached out, took her hand and brought it to his lips. Kissing the back of her hand, then her palm, and still holding it close to his mouth, he said, "Remember that, *mio moglie,* will you—" his eyes bored into her "—in the days to come."

He let her hand go, then set his gaze on his son, who sat quietly watching him. "You were a good boy at the church, *figlio.* Thank you." He dipped his head and whispered something in Nicci's ear. Something that made Nicci smile and turn to look back at Rhea.

Rhea was curious about what Joey had said to

elicit such a wide smile, but she decided she would wait to ask Nicci. Wait until they were home and the day had passed.

Joey said, "Norman is going to hold you for your *madre* once we get outside. You let him, and listen to what he tells you. It's important, *figlio. Capiche?"*

Nicci nodded once, still smiling. *"Capiche."*

Joey embraced his son, kissed him on both cheeks, then opened the door. Once he was out of the car, he handed Nicci to Norman, then he reached back inside and enclosed Rhea's cold hand in his. "Come, darlin'. Let's finish this, so *mio padre* can finally rest in peace."

By the time they reached Frank's grave site, the cemetery was packed with cars and a large group had gathered. After they had taken their places under the tented pavilion, Rhea scanned faces, relieved when she located Jackson, Sunni and Lavina. Remembering what Joey had told her in the car, she studied the crowd, trying to make out who the feds were—an impossible task.

Movement directly across from them drew her attention, and her eyes met those of the man responsible for tearing all their lives apart. She had worked hard not to hate Stud for all he'd done. She had tried to understand his torment, and to some degree she had, but as she looked at Carlo Talupa, she couldn't hold back the hate that surfaced. He was an evil man, even though his grandfatherly appearance contradicted that fact. And that was the irony. The travesty, Rhea decided.

He was a little bent, and his skin was wrinkled, his cheeks saggy. He was dressed in a long navy-blue coat, his brimmed fedora making his ears stick out. He didn't have cold eyes, but Rhea knew he had the coldest heart of any man alive.

Four bodyguards flanked him and six more guards covered his back. That in itself bore witness to how much the man was hated.

The rumors were that he'd put out more contracts across the country, and had been responsible for more mob hits, than any other crime boss in Chicago. That thought sent a raw chill through Rhea, knowing the cemetery could turn into a war zone at any moment.

Joey must have sensed Rhea's rising panic, because he reached over, curled his hand around hers and squeezed.

She glanced behind and to the left of Carlo Talupa, to see Sophia D'Lano. She stood next to a squat, ruddy-faced man with a wide, flat nose and a mustache that covered his entire mouth. She saw his mustache move, then Sophia said something in reply. Seconds later the man on Sophia's right laughed.

Rhea had been reading the newspapers since she'd returned to Chicago. The laughing man was Moody Trafano, Sophia's half brother. He was tall and slender, his hair lighter than her own, which made him look ridiculously out of place in the sea of black-haired Sicilians. Absently, Rhea wondered if she looked as out of place as Moody Trafano did. Vincent D'Lano's bastard son may as well have been branded with a *B* on his forehead.

She glanced at Lucky, who stood next to Joey. Unlike Joey and Jackson, he had rejected the customary black suit and black coat. He wore jeans and a dark red sweater beneath a three-quarter length scarred brown leather jacket that had definitely seen a number of wars. Their eyes met and held only a moment.

In less than twenty-four hours, Rhea's opinion of Lucky had completely changed. She had always been wary of Joey's younger brother, but no longer. He'd surprised her last night, welcoming her into the family the way he had done. The sincerity in his eyes had overwhelmed her, and the gentle touch he'd offered Nicci had clearly told her that, like his brother, there was more to Lucky Masado than met the eye.

Once more Rhea felt as if she were being dissected, and she scanned the crowd again, to find Sophia D'Lano glaring at her. Outfitted in a silver fur coat and a matching fur hat, Sophia looked like the reigning queen of the kingdom—the mafia kingdom. Her hostility was so tangible that Rhea could almost feel the knives from Sophia's black eyes being tossed at her.

It was during the closing prayer that a long black limousine entered the cemetery and cruised around the loop, moving at a snail's pace. Rhea saw Lucky slowly shift his body, saw his hand slide inside his jacket. Joey let go of her hand and did the same.

The black limo pulled off the road in full view of the grave site, but no one got out. The priest stepped back, his eyes on Joey. Suddenly Joey stepped forward, a knife appearing in his hand so quickly that Rhea wasn't sure where it had come from. He cut two bloodred roses off the enormous spray that draped the casket, brought them to his lips, then kissed the petals. Seconds later, he handed one of the roses to her and the other to their son.

The act set off a steady hum that went through the crowd. Joey had just announced to the *famiglia* that he had a son—a son he acknowledged—as well as a wife.

As the mourners started to disperse, two gunshots were fired into the crowd. Screams went up, and Rhea was shoved forward against the cold casket. Then came the words "Stay down!"

She turned her head as Lucky dwarfed her with his body. Paralyzed with fear, she glanced sideways, anxious to locate Nicci. She saw Joey grab their son from Norman, and then, as if Norman Gates had gone through the drill a hundred times, he made himself into a human shield for Joey and they quickly moved toward the limousine.

Another volley of shots rang out and a spray of snow flashed around Joey's and Norman's feet as they ran. The second Rhea saw how close the shots were, she cried out and tried to run after them. Lucky grabbed her and tossed her behind him, cussing anxiously. Obviously he was as aware as she was that Joey could be shot in the back at any minute.

Rhea demanded, "Go, Lucky. Go to Joey."

He snapped his head around. "*Non posso!* I won't leave you!"

"You have to! Joey and Nicci need you. I'll stay here. I'll be all right. Go now!"

"*Maledizione!* Don't move, and stay down." Lucky pushed her to her knees. Then he was running and dodging the screaming crowd to reach Joey, as gunshot continued to follow them to the limousine.

A wild bullet blew the corner off Frank's casket, and Rhea sought cover in the open grave. No longer able to see if Joey and Nicci had made it safely to the car, she bit her lip and hovered in the hole as more gunfire ricocheted off the casket overhead.

Minutes passed, and still the shrieks and shots continued. Then, out of nowhere, a hand reached down, grabbed her arm and lifted her out of the hole.

Ordered to run, Rhea took off with her head low, determined to keep up with the long stride that was setting the pace and pulling her along.

She didn't realize until it was too late that she was running in the wrong direction.

Mayhem could be a great diversion, the key to any successful plan. And now that he had gotten what he came for, and it was safely tucked away in the trunk of his limousine, Vito rapped on the window and ordered his driver to return to Dante Armanno.

On the order, the long black stretch cruised out of Rosewood Cemetery's iron gates as slowly as it had entered. No one paid any attention; shots were still being fired and the confusion appeared to be growing.

Vito smiled as he watched two of his men behind a gravestone raise their rifles and turn up the heat with another round of gunfire.

It had been worth it to humble himself and ask Summ to dress him, Vito decided. From there, he'd ordered two of his guards to help him outside and into his car. And that, too, had been worth surrendering his pride. Yes, a thousand times worth it. The humiliation of having a woman wiggle his shorts up his legs and over his gone-to-fat belly no longer stung so much. Nor did it bother him that he'd needed to lean on Benito, his most trusted bodyguard, to make it to the car.

"I want you to write a letter to Kendler, Summ."

"Now, *Shujin?*"

"I said so, didn't I?"

Bundled into a green shawl, Summ sat across from him with her head slightly bowed. But Vito knew damn well she had seen everything from the moment the first shot had been fired. Her humble actions didn't fool him a bit. She was about as obedient and innocent as a mosquito, and twice as busy.

She opened her cloth bag and took out a pen and paper. "It is good, your decision," she said.

"So now you approve of my vengeance? After preaching forgiveness for twenty years, you suddenly have taken up the sword?" Vito groused.

"It is not vengeance you seek, but justice, *Shujin.*"

Vito snorted, then puffed on his Italian cigar. "Now you know what I'm thinking, too?"

She didn't answer, and in the silence, Vito glanced back at the pavilion where the silver casket covered in red roses shimmered in the snow. He hadn't expected the pang of regret that assailed him, or the thickening in his throat. His old friend was dead. His friend and enemy.

It was too late for regrets, he reminded himself. Useless to conjure up memories of the past. A waste of effort to dwell on happy times. But there *had* been happy times with Frank. He had simply pushed them aside years ago, along with his thoughts of Grace. After reliving the good memories, what followed was a nightmare.

The words *what if* suddenly entered his thoughts, and Vito muttered, "I've waited years to see Frank Masado dead. I expected to feel better once it was done."

As the limo left the cemetery, Summ said, "Perhaps time has healed the open wound."

Again Vito snorted. "Or maybe it's your witch's

brew that has turned my head to mush, and I'm no
longer thinking straight.''

He had to admit it was a powerful concoction, her
stinky tea. It had to be, for him to still be alive.
Summ's herbal remedies and holistic ideas had kept
him from death's door when expensive medicines
had failed. His doctors were amazed. His cancer was
full-blown and hungry. He should have died months
ago. And it was inevitable that he would die. But
how soon depended upon Summ, not on modern
medicine.

''Are you ready to write?'' he asked, not liking it
when he thought too much about Summ. He'd grown
to care for the mouthy little witch. She'd become his
nurse, his mistress and his counselor. Whatever he
had needed, she had delivered, and it saddened him
that he wouldn't be able to take her with him where
he was going. Maybe he was even a little afraid to
be going without her—she had become so much a
part of him. His lifeline at a time when he thought
he'd been forsaken.

Vito Tandi…afraid. Not to die, he silently avowed,
but he wished there was a way to know if it all would
work out as it should. Had all of their paths been
predestined?

''I was wondering if you would like me to ask
Buddha for a favor on your behalf.''

Vito narrowed his eyes, sure that Summ had just
read his thoughts. Why else would she have asked
such a question? ''My God wrote me off years ago.

Why would yours give a damn about granting me a favor?''

"Because my heart is pure and my motives equally so. Buddha grants gifts to those who are pure in heart, even if those gifts are extended to another. Even if it is extended to an old fool too proud and stubborn to ask for himself.''

"There are days, Summ, that I wonder why I rescued you from that alley in Chinatown where you were scavenging for food. Write the letter, witch.''

She bent her head and raised her pen. "Dear Mr. Kendler,'' she began.

"He's not dear to me. Start again. Just 'Kendler.' Tell him I want him at Dante Armanno at nine in the morning.''

Her hand stilled and she looked up. "At nine?''

"Are you deaf? Maybe you should be drinking some of that godawful tea you've been pouring down my throat for months. It's suppose to work miracles, right? Maybe it'll melt the wax in your ears.''

"I hear fine, *Shujin*. But you haven't been up by nine in over a year.''

Scowling, Vito grumbled, "Tomorrow I will be up at nine. Kendler is to meet me in my office to change my will.'' He poked his fat finger at the paper. "Add that if it takes the entire day to rewrite my will, he should be prepared to bring a sack lunch. Lawyers are the whores of this crazy society. They jump from one poor bastard to another without conscience or shame, and I refuse to feed him.''

"Change your will? But I thought—"

"Don't worry, Summ. I wouldn't think of burdening you with the task of managing Dante Armanno after I'm gone. You'd probably burn my millions in the fireplace to save on next year's heating bill. But you won't be leaving as we once discussed. I've decided to shake up the *famiglia*, and let them all know that Vito Tandi's brain hasn't rotted along with his body. I will be remembered, even from the grave. Remembered as the man who brought honor back to the *Cosa Nostra.*"

Joey ignored the blood that soaked his shirt. He had broke open his shoulder wound, but he didn't give a damn about that. Rhea was missing, and he had already taken Lucky apart for leaving her unprotected.

"She's got to be with one of the guards, Joe," Jackson reasoned. "She'll show up. Just give it a little more time. It's been barely an hour."

It was true. One of his guards could have picked Rhea up—but Joey's instincts told him that hadn't happened. Over half of his men had called to check in with nothing to report except that they were alive. And when he had asked them about Rhea, none could give him any information.

"Tell me again what you know, Jacky," Joey said roughly.

"Carlo got away. I don't know how that could

have happened, but he slipped through the feds' fingers.''

Joey swore. ''Carlo's missing, and so is Rhea. What does that tell you, Jacky?''

''Don't jump to conclusions, *fratello*.''

Joey turned to glare at Lucky, who stood behind the bar with a glass of scotch in one hand and a bag of ice in the other pressed to his cheek. He'd been drinking nonstop since they learned that Rhea was nowhere to be found. It went without saying that Lucky blamed himself for her disappearance, and it hadn't helped any that Joey had taken a punch at him the minute he realized his brother had left his Rhea without protection.

''The feds did pick up Carmine Solousi. If he decides to talk, we—''

''He won't talk,'' Lucky said. ''Not unless they get Carlo. If they don't find him soon, I can guarantee that that bookie who was ready to sing in Allenwood will be dead within twenty-four hours, too.''

Joey stepped behind the bar and pushed past Lucky. After he opened the hidden door, he walked into the passageway. When Lucky and Jackson followed, he said, ''I can't sit around here doing nothing. I want my wife, and if that means I have to storm Carlo's estate, then that's what I'll do.''

''That's suicide, Joe,'' Jackson growled.

Joey reached for a matched pair of Berettas, then a box of ammo. Next, he pulled the shotgun his father had given him at age fifteen off the wall, an exact duplicate to the Italian *lupara* Lucky owned.

On his way back out the door, he grabbed the leather coat that hung on a hook; it was equipped with enough pockets inside the lining to house his banquet of serious toys. Back in the living room, he jerked off his suit jacket, ignored his bloodstained white shirt, and pulled on the coat. After sliding the *lupara* into one of the lining pockets, he transferred his knife and one of the Berettas into the right outside pocket, and the other Beretta and his cell phone into the left.

"Joey, you need to stop and think about this." Lucky blocked his brother's path as he headed for the door.

"Get out of my way, Lucky."

"No. You're going to get yourself killed. That won't help Rhea."

When Joey tried to go around Lucky, his brother gave him a push and he fell against Jackson, who quickly grabbed his arms and pulled them behind his back to restrain him. Joey swore, then fought to free himself. He threw his weight, sent Jackson off balance, and both of them fell to the floor in a scuffle.

"Dammit, Joey." Lucky reached down and hauled his brother back to his feet. As Jackson scrambled up off the floor, he threw a punch to Joey's midsection that momentarily stole his air. The lapse in time gave Lucky the opportunity he needed to pin Joey against the bar. "*Basta!* Enough, Joey."

A cell phone rang, and for a moment no one moved, then Lucky let Joey go.

Jackson flipped open his phone. "Ward here, what do you got?" After a few minutes, he pocketed the phone. "That was Hank Mallory at the CPD. He says Carlo never went back to his estate. He's either left the city or gone underground."

Joey shoved away from the bar. He had never felt so helpless in all of his life. Helpless and scared.

"There's more, Joe." Jackson hesitated, then said, "The limousine that entered the cemetery just before hell broke loose belongs to Vito Tandi."

Lucky asked, "Why would Vito show up at Frank's funeral?"

"Good question. Something we need to ask Vito," Joey answered.

"Dante Armanno is guarded like Fort Knox, Joe."

Joey knew what Jackson said was true, but he didn't care. He couldn't sit around and do nothing. "Opal!"

The nanny hurried into the living room carrying Niccolo. "Yes, Mr. Masado."

"We're going out. Stay with my son. Don't leave him for even a second."

Chapter 11

Rhea lifted her head and slowly rolled to her back. Her head throbbed, and when she raised her hand to push her hair out of her eyes, her hand came away wet and sticky.

Carefully, she ran her fingers along her temple to see how badly she was bleeding. She discovered an inch-long cut running from her temple back to her hairline. She closed her eyes and tried to remember what had happened. She'd been running with the guard, and then as they had reached the limousine....

She didn't remember if the guard had turned back and punched her, or if someone else had suddenly come up behind her. All she remembered was that the force of the punch had knocked the wind out of her and she'd dropped to her knees. The next thing she remembered was being tossed into the trunk of the limousine, hitting her head on something sharp. She was still in the trunk. She could feel the motion and hear the tires as the car sped along the street. Smell the exhaust.

The question was, why would one of Joey's guards want to hurt her?

He wouldn't, Rhea decided, blinking her eyes open and staring into the darkness. The second she came to that realization, fear sent a wave of nausea climbing up her throat.

Had Carlo Talupa managed to elude the feds? Had he somehow learned they were going to arrest him, and before that could happen, had he extracted yet another calculated hit on the Masado family?

If that was true, then she was in the worst situation possible. She had seen what Carlo had done to Grace. The boss of the *famiglia* was a sadist. If he had her, what kind of torture did he have planned?

The car slowed down, then came to a stop. Rhea heard the sound of the car door slamming, then whistling. She started to shake when she heard footsteps and the rattle of keys.

She held her breath, prayed she was wrong.

When the trunk opened, a beam of light shone into the darkness and there was no longer any mystery as to who had pulled her from the open grave. No mystery as to what her fate would be. Rhea recognized her captor clearly.

* * *

Dante Armanno looked like a medieval fortress. Dark and sheltered by iron gates and giant oak trees, the three-story home of Vito Tandi had a parapet on the rooftop and witches towers extending from three sides.

The estate had been built in 1918. High on the hillside overlooking the Chicago River, the design and placement of the house in conjunction with the road guaranteed that the guards stationed on the roof could see every car that came within two miles of the estate.

As Joey drove up to the iron gates, he saw that Lucky was already there. Looking like the dark side of evil, his brother was talking to two guards with AR-70's strapped on their shoulders.

"Give him a minute," Jackson said. "If anyone can convince these hard cases to let us in, it'll be Lucky."

Joey planned to give his brother no more than two minutes. Then he was going to run the guards down, if that was the only way he would get to speak to Vito.

When the iron gates opened Joey wasted no time speeding through. A quarter mile up the road, and through a second gate, he turned onto a paved circle drive with a massive bronze statue standing in the middle. The statue was of Dante Armanno.

Joey muttered, "The last standing soldier."

"What?" Jackson asked.

"The statue of Armanno," Joey explained. "He's the Sicilian soldier in the story of how the *Cosa Nostra* came to be in Sicily."

"He looks like a mean son of a bitch."

Joey nodded. "He was. That's how he got his name. Dante Armanno means last standing soldier." Joey spotted the guards on the parapet. "Watch your back, Jacky. I don't want to get anyone pissed off. If Vito has Rhea, I don't want her paying for another one of my mistakes. I've made too damn many already."

"You didn't make a mistake, Joe. You couldn't be in two places at once." Jackson eyed the rooftop. "We must be crazy walking into the lion's den. You ever been here before?"

"No. Never been invited." Joey climbed out from behind the wheel of his Jaguar. As he waited for Lucky to pull up in the blue company van from Masado Towers, he studied another pair of statues, hungry-looking black panthers sitting in front of the house on granite plinths. The house's mullion windows were long and narrow, an architectural design that prevented unwanted entry through a broken window. That is, if you were able to get past the gate, and then the giant who stood at the door.

"Name's Benito Palone," Lucky said as he joined them. "He's been with Vito for about ten years."

They started toward the house, walking side by side through a keystone archway that extended sixteen feet up and led to the vault-like front door—

Joey in the middle, Lucky on his left and Jackson on his right.

"The story is, Palone's got a steel plate in his jaw," Lucky muttered as they closed the distance on the seven-foot-plus guard.

Joey called out, "I've come to speak with Vito."

"Do you have an appointment?" said the giant.

"You know damn well that I don't," Joey growled.

Lucky said, "He'll want to see us, Palone."

"Maybe. Wait here."

He disappeared inside, and was gone only a minute. When he returned, a small oriental woman was with him. She sized up the three of them, then said, "*Shujin* say leave weapons here." She motioned to a marble slab tucked back into an alcove. "They will be there when you leave."

Joey had never seen Vito's housekeeper, but if you could believe the rumors, this small woman had managed to keep Tandi alive for the past two years when the doctors had given up.

He pulled his two Berettas along with the *lupara* that he'd tucked into the deep pocket of his long coat while Lucky did the same. Jackson was slow to give up his Diamondback, but he finally laid it on the marble slab with the other weapons.

The woman pointed to Lucky. "You keep a .22 in a hip pocket, and I don't see the knives." She pointed to where the guns had been laid. "You waste time."

Joey reached into his pocket and gave up his Hibben, and Lucky and Jackson followed suit. Then Lucky anted up his .22 in his back pocket.

"*Shujin* in study. Come."

They followed her through the door, and when it closed, they were joined by two heavily armed guards and Palone, who followed them through the foyer and down a hall that swung left. The dark hall was spotlighted by several shadow boxes displaying antique guns and knives that were more than a century old.

Another guard was standing outside an ornately carved wooden door. The guard knocked twice, then he shoved open the door and Joey, Jackson and Lucky stepped inside. Palone followed close behind.

Vito's study was as dimly lit as the hall. Joey scanned the room and found his father's old friend and enemy seated at a large wooden desk. Not having seen Vito for many years, Joey was surprised that he was bald and at least sixty pounds overweight.

He simply asked, "Where's my wife?"

"Your wife? I wasn't aware you had a wife, Joey."

"You were at the cemetery today. You know damn well what went on there. My wife is missing."

Vito puffed on his cigar, studying first Joey, then Lucky. Giving Jackson only a quick glance, he said, "It's been a helluva week, eh, boys? First Frank, and now your wife. I sympathize. I know what it feels like to lose family. My wife years ago, and then Milo a few months back. Yes, a helluva week for you boys.''

Joey clenched his fists. He was ready to climb over the desk, when he felt Lucky's hand on his arm.

"Easy, *fratello*." To Vito, he said, "The past cannot be altered, old man. We are interested in the present. What is your price to hand over Rhea Masado?"

Vito shrugged. "If I had her, I'm sure there would be something. But I'm sorry to say I don't have your wife, Joey."

At that moment Jackson's cell phone rang. Joey heard him back away to answer.

Jackson spoke low, for only a minute at the most, and when the phone was back in his pocket, he said, "Joe, we need to talk."

"Not now, Jacky," Joey said roughly.

"*Now,* Joe."

The tone in his friend's voice made Joey whirl around, and when he saw the sick look on Jackson's face, his gut twisted. Leaving Lucky with Vito and Palone, Joey walked out the door with Jackson on his heels. In the hall, he asked, "What the hell is it, Jacky?"

"That was Hank. He just got a call from Joliet Prison. Stud Williams escaped this morning."

The words hit Joey as if a land mine had gone off inside his head.

"They have a woman fitting Sophia D'Lano's de-

scription on the visitors schedule,'' Jackson went on.
"She met with Stud Williams two days ago.''

Joey's entire body started to shake and he leaned
against the wall for support.

"Breathe, Joe,'' Jackson ordered. "It looks like
Vito's telling the truth. Ten to one, Stud was at the
cemetery, and when he saw his chance he took it.
What do you think?''

"I think I'm going to kill him this time.''

"Where would he take her, Joe?''

Joey thought a minute, his mind racing. "Not back
to his house, or to her old place. That would be too
obvious. He'll go underground, or clear out alto-
gether. If Sophia's involved, then so is her old man.''

"Remember when Frank said Carlo and Vito took
him and Grace to a cabin north of here? Up by
Waukegan somewhere. He said it was Vinnie
D'Lano's place, right? What do you think? Plenty of
woods. No neighbors.''

Jackson's description of the place sickened Joey.
He shoved away from the wall. "It's a place to
start.''

He returned to Vito's study. Without wasting any
more time, he said, "I've just learned that Stud Williams escaped from prison today. You remember
him, don't you, Vito? He's the dirty cop who murdered Milo. Tied him down and shot him in the
head.'' When Joey saw Vito's nostrils flare, he said,
"I need to know where Vincent D'Lano's cabin is.
The one you and Carlo brought my father to the night

you took his eye, then beat the hell out of him with a steel pipe.''

Vito Tandi's eyes narrowed. "Williams is out?'' He swore crudely. "I want that bastard.''

"Pick a number and get in line,'' Jackson countered.

Vito said, "If I help you, I'll expect a favor.''

"What kind of favor?'' Joey asked.

"I need to give it some thought. I'll decide that later, but if you agree—'' he looked from Lucky to Joey ''—I'll provide you with everything you need to run down the scum who murdered my son. I have a helicopter here. You can leave immediately and reach the cabin in less than an hour.''

Joey glanced at his watch, calculated the time. If Stud had Rhea, and there was a good chance that he did, she had been with him for over two hours. Ten minutes with her bastard ex-husband was too long, he mused.

"Do we have a deal, boys?''

"*Si,*'' Joey said. "We have a deal.''

Vito looked at Lucky. "Do you agree with your *fratello,* Tomas?''

"*Si,* old man. We have a deal.''

Rhea felt as if a nail had been driven through her skull. She shouldn't have fought him, but she had reacted on instinct. Instinct and fear.

It was painful to open her eyes, but she made an

effort. She squinted, fighting the light overhead that was causing her to see black dots and hazy colors.

She was lying flat on her back. On a bed, she thought. Her arms were stretched over her head, and her wrists were bound and tied to something sturdy. She could barely lift her head, it hurt so bad. Still she gritted her teeth and twisted her neck to see that her wrists had been tied to the iron frame of the bed with a leather belt.

"It's been a long time, honey. Too long."

The voice made Rhea shudder. She heard movement, a chair creak, and then her ex-husband was standing beside the bed, staring down at her.

"Stud? I thought..."

"I was behind bars? Nothing can keep me from you, honey. You should know that by now. You're what I live for."

Rhea studied her ex-husband. He was dressed all in black like a bodyguard. That's why she hadn't recognized him, she decided. He'd fooled her into thinking he was one of Joey's men.

His blue eyes looked bloodshot, which meant he was drinking. Had been for a while. She glanced at his blond hair, thinking the military short cut made him look even more frightening than before.

He reached out and brushed her hair out of her eyes. "You look good, honey. Real good."

His hand drifted to her cheek, and she tried to turn her face away, but his rough fingers dug in and pinched hard.

Rhea gasped and closed her eyes.

"I could snap your neck," he threatened, then bent forward and brushed his lips over her mouth. "But you know I won't."

Suddenly he let go of her cheek, leaving behind a pulsing ache. Rhea drew in a shaky breath and exhaled slowly, and that's when he struck again, closing one hand over her nose and the other over her mouth.

The sick game slammed Rhea back into the nightmares of her past, and her eyes widened out of fear and the knowledge of what was coming next. She knew better than to struggle, but her lungs were almost out of air. She started to panic, to twist on the bed and raise her legs to kick at him. But like always, he was too strong, and too determined to have his fun.

Just when Rhea thought she would pass out, he let go of her and stepped back. Dizzy, she gulped air, desperate to feed her starved lungs.

"You're out of practice, honey. You used to be able to last longer."

Rhea refused to cry. She wanted to, but tears only fed Stud's sickness. He loved the games, loved it when he could completely break her—when she was shattered both physically and emotionally.

It always started this way, the pinching and choking. What followed after that…Rhea didn't want to think about. It was all part of Stud's own special recipe for terror.

Suddenly he was back, leaning over her, pinching her mouth together, squeezing hard enough to force Rhea to whimper.

"I know why you ran off. I know about your kid. About Joey Masado. That kid should have been mine." Abruptly he let her go. "It's too bad I wasn't able to get my hands on the little bastard at the cemetery. I had planned to bring him along so he could watch us play our games."

Rhea groaned. The very idea of Nicci being subjected to Stud's insanity made her sick. She rolled her head to the side and saw a bottle of whiskey on the nightstand.

He was so predictable. He would drink now. Sit and brood, and let the rage build inside him until it forced him into another outburst.

Rhea tried not to think about the next time, and turned her thoughts to Nicci and Joey, praying that they were safe. "I'm going to teach you a lesson, honey," he taunted from his chair. "This time I'm going to make it clear just who owns you. You're my wife. Mine! I plan on beating that fact into you so you never forget it."

Rhea turned to see Stud raise the whiskey bottle to his lips. Seconds later, he said, "We're going to take a little trip, honey."

Trip. Rhea's instincts screamed, *No!* But then, traveling would keep Stud's hands busy, and as long as she could stay healthy, there was a small chance she might be able to escape.

"We're starting over, honey…you and me. You're going to give me what you gave Masado." Suddenly he was again standing by the bed, one hand moving to cover her nose and the other reaching for her throat. "I'll have a son who looks like me. Me! Not that black-haired Sicilian. For better or worse, Rhea. That's what you promised. That's what I promised, too."

Vito's pilot landed the helicopter at the Waukegan Airport. Vincent D'Lano's cabin was less than ten miles away, and the reed-thin pilot led them to a black Blazer. They climbed in, and as the driver cruised the back roads as if he were still flying, Jackson discussed strategy, Lucky checked their ammo and Joey chain-smoked and stared out the window.

Fifteen minutes later they parked by the side of the road and got out of the car. It was obvious the cabin was empty. But it was also clear that it had been used recently—there was evidence that someone had been restrained on the bed in the back bedroom.

Joey turned away, sick at the sight of the rumpled bedding and the leather belt left dangling from the iron headboard. He heard Lucky swear behind him, then heard the front door slam as his brother left the cabin.

After searching the grounds, Jackson said, "I called Hank Mallory. He says a silver Lexus was reported stolen in the vicinity of Rosewood Cemetery this afternoon. He says the car was sighted on I-94, headed toward Milwaukee about thirty minutes ago, but the driver managed to avoid their blockade and they haven't seen him since.''

As they piled back into the black Blazer, Lucky took the wheel, telling Vito's driver, ''I'll take it from here, Slim. You damn near rolled us on that S-turn five miles back.''

Six small towns and two hours later, and gambling on a hunch, Joey spotted the silver Lexus parked in front of room four at the Sleepy Hollow Motel in Sternsberg, Wisconsin.

Lucky said, ''How do you want to do this, *fratello?* We going in quiet, or noisy?''

Joey had had fifty miles to contemplate how he was going to rip Stud Williams's head off. There would be no warnings, no wasted minutes contemplating the situation. Too much time had gone by already. He checked his watch.

''Rhea's been in Williams's hands for almost six hours. There's a chance she's hurt. We go in noisy.''

''Noisy it is.'' Jackson pulled his Diamondback from his back pocket, while Lucky reached for the *lupara* that sat between the seats.

Joey leapt from the Blazer. ''On three,'' he said. ''I'll fire a shot to get things started.'' Then he slipped out of sight.

They had played the suffocation game twice in the motel. Rhea had passed out the second time. Now awake, she assessed her surroundings.

As much as she tried to stay alert, Stud's games were slowly draining her. The only good thing she could see in all of this was that they were moving farther away from Chicago, and that meant Stud wouldn't be able to hurt Nicci.

She was on the bed again, only this time Stud hadn't tied her. Not yet, anyway. She could hear the TV, and smell the old room's stale air mixed with the sweet odor of whiskey.

She willed her body not to move—not even a muscle. If she could fool Stud into thinking that she was still unconscious, she would have time to regain some of her strength.

At first she had thought that if she lived through the night, tomorrow she would attempt to escape. But now, untied, all she had to do was wait for Stud to fall asleep, then run.

It was while Rhea was lying as still as death and praying for Stud to fall asleep, that an explosion outside rocked the motel. She wasn't sure where it came from, or what it was. But it had been close—close enough to rattle the windows.

She heard Stud curse, and she raised her head in time to see him scramble to his feet. His eyes were puffy, his shirt unbuttoned and his pants half unzipped. He looked confused but aware that something was definitely wrong.

She rolled to her side and sat up just as another explosion, more violent than the first, shook the motel's foundation. Then suddenly the three-foot-square window next to the bed shattered.

For an instant Rhea thought it had shattered from the explosion, but then a body came sailing through the opening cloaked in a leather coat, and she understood.

Joey had come for her.

She glanced at Stud, saw him reach for the gun on the table, and she cried out as she scrambled off the bed. Seconds later, the front door flew off its hinges and Lucky came through, followed by Jackson Ward.

Rhea glanced back to Joey, who was already on Stud. She heard him roar like a raging bull, heard Stud howl in pain as Joey sent his fist into his face, the force lifting Stud off his feet.

She backed up against the wall as Stud dragged himself back to his feet. He still had his gun, but not for long. Joey raised his leg and kicked out, sending Stud flying into the table. Stud let go of the gun as he squealed in pain, and this time he didn't get up.

It was all over within minutes. Joey spun around, searching for Rhea. When he found her against the wall, the question in his eyes was obvious.

In a raspy voice, Rhea said, "I'm all right. Nicci… where is he? Is he—"

"He's safe at home."

"Dammit, Joey!"

The angry voice was Lucky's, and it sent Rhea's attention to the doorway, where Joey's brother stood with his hands on his hips, his *lupara* slung over his shoulder. He was eyeing the situation with a scowl on his face. Finally, he said, "I thought we agreed to go in on the count of three."

Joey shrugged. "One. Two. Three… What difference does it make?"

"The difference is he could have drilled you coming through the window."

Lucky stepped inside, and as he passed Stud he gave the man a solid kick to his midsection to ensure he stayed down, then retrieved the .38 on the floor and pocketed it.

Behind him, Jackson entered the room with jaw set and eyes narrowed. It was a fact—he had as good a reason as anyone to hate Stud Williams. Stud had killed Jackson's partner three years ago, and a few weeks back, he'd terrorized Sunni and almost killed her. Still, believing in the old adage *Never hit a man when he's down,* Jackson waited until Stud got to his knees before he sent him to the floor again with a hard-driving right that broke the man's jaw.

Rhea watched Joey come toward her, his eyes fixed on her bruised neck and the cut on her temple. He said, "Do you need a doctor?"

She shook her head, then said, "No. I'm not seriously hurt."

He reached out and gently touched the bruise on her cheek. Rhea angled her head and closed her eyes, needing to feel his contained strength. Softly, she whispered, "I'm all right. He never…touched me."

Behind them, Lucky said, "I told Slim to get you a motel room at the Pink Peacock. It's across the street. Take a few hours. We'll clean up this mess."

Joey pulled Rhea close and wrapped his arm around her, and they headed to the door. Rhea caught Lucky staring at her, and she read guilt in his eyes. She stopped, slipped away from Joey and walked straight to Lucky. Sliding her arms around his hard waist, she hugged him, and when his arms came around her and hugged her back, she said, "Nicci's home safe. That might not have been the case if you hadn't gone to him and Joey. Thank you for that, *mio fratello.*" Then on tiptoes she kissed both of his cheeks.

Behind her, Jackson draped her coat around her shoulders, and then she went out the door with Joey.

The air was cold and it made Rhea shiver. Suddenly Joey lifted her into his arms, and as she tucked her face into the warm curve of his neck, he crossed the street, ignoring the crowd that had gathered.

Rhea hadn't shed a tear in five hours, but now the tears flowed freely, wetting Joey's shirt.

Close to her ear, he said, "You sure you don't need a doctor, darlin'?"

"No," she sobbed softly. "All I need is you."

Chapter 12

Twelve hours had passed since Joey had rescued Rhea from the Sleepy Hollow Motel and her ex-husband's mania. As he and Lucky entered the back room of the Stardust, he saw that Jackson and Police Chief Hank Mallory were already there waiting for them.

Taking a seat at the circular table, Joey nodded to Jackson, then said to Hank Mallory, "Did you get him? Did you get Carlo Talupa?"

"No. There's still no sign of him yet. It's like he just vanished," Hank conceded. "That's a concern, so my advice for you and Lucky is to lay low for a while until we've got him in custody."

Joey swore.

Lucky said nothing.

"Stud Williams is being held in the county jail until he can be transferred back to Joliet. Jackson's agreed to work with me on gathering what we need to make an arrest on Vincent D'Lano and his daughter, Sophia. As soon as we can confirm their involvement in Williams's prison break we'll pick them up."

"That'll be sooner than you think, Joe," Jackson added. "Two days at the most is my guess."

Hank stubbed out his cigarette in the ashtray in front of him. His thirty years of experience with the Chicago Police Department showed in the age lines surrounding his blue eyes and his receding gray hair. Leaning forward in his dark suit and white shirt, his gaze moved from Joey to Lucky. "Now that Talupa's made some serious mistakes, and we're in a better position to benefit from them, things are going to move faster from here on out."

"Maybe. Then again, maybe not," Joey interrupted. "We'll have to wait and see. You haven't got Carlo yet."

"That sounds like you're having second thoughts. If we're going to have any success in our joint coalition, you two, as undercover informants, are going to need to be with me and Jackson on this a hundred percent. I'd need to know right now if that poses a problem for either of you."

Joey eyed his brother. "Lucky?"

Lucky leaned back in his chair, his scarred hand turning a pencil over and over between two of his long fingers. Finally, he said, "We made a deal a few days ago, Mallory. I don't usually make deals with cops. That should tell you that I didn't make this one lightly, or without considering its outcome. Joey and I agreed to this, and we intend to stick by our decision. If you want to call us undercover informants, that's your choice. Only that's not who we are, or what this is about for us. It's not about squealing on our *amigos*. We want to nail men like Carlo and the other fat dogs who have forgotten what it means to be a true *soldato* in the brotherhood. It's about another kind of justice for us, Mallory."

"I respect your view on it, Lucky. I know this deal wasn't easy for either of you to make. I understand why you did it and I know I'm asking for a lot here. Betraying friends—"

"We're not betraying anyone. As I said, the fat dogs have become gluttons. They taint our honor and blacken our respect. On Sicilian soil such a man would lose his head for being a *Venduto*. They are the traitors and betrayers. Not my *fratello,* or myself."

Joey shoved his chair away from the table and stood. Slowly he moved to stand behind Lucky. Resting his hands on his brother's shoulders, he said, "We are in this together." His gaze found Jackson. "My brothers, and I."

His meaning clear, Mallory nodded. "Good. Then we can move forward."

Joey said, "You have done what you said you

would do for us, and we are grateful. That gratitude
will be proven as soon as you find Carlo. Keep him
behind bars long enough, and we will get you what
you need to keep him there. Only then will our coalition move forward.''

"We'll stay in touch." Hank Mallory checked his
watch, then stood. "It's almost noon, and I've got
another meeting at one." He glanced at Jackson.
"How about having lunch with me out front? Then
you can tell me more about this wedding date you
and Sunni have set. Why anyone would want to get
married on New Year's Day is beyond me."

Jackson climbed out of his chair. To Joey and
Lucky, he said, "If it were me, I'd take a little trip.
A week should do it."

"We're already ahead of you, Jacky," Joey said.
"We'll be gone by morning."

After Jackson and Mallory left, Joey said to
Lucky, "I never thanked you for what you did last
night."

Lucky arched a black brow. "I need no thanks,
Joey."

Joey eyed the vivid bruise on Lucky's cheek. "I
lost my head. I turned into—"

"A hailstorm on wheels, I think are the words
you're looking for." Lucky stared at this brother for
a long time. Then he snapped the pencil in two and
handed Joey one of the pieces. "You and me, we're
two halves of the same creation, *fratello*. What Frank
taught you, he taught me, too. Make no mistake,

Joey, we think alike, and sometimes even act very much alike. If roles had been reversed yesterday, and the woman that I loved had been taken from me, I would have done the same as you did.'' He touched his discolored cheek, then grinned. ''Then again, maybe I wouldn't have stopped after just one punch. *Capiche?*''

''I don't understand,'' Rhea said. ''We're taking a trip?''

Joey had just told her that they were flying to Santa Palazzo. That they were going to disappear for a few days.

''I thought it was too dangerous to fly there. What if someone follows us? What if—''

''Carlo will be too busy trying to stay out of the hands of the feds to worry about us right now. It's a perfect time to leave Chicago. A perfect time for you to spend a few days with Elena and Grace. I'll keep in touch with Jacky. We've already got it all worked out.''

''But—''

''You want to see Grace and Elena, don't you?''

Of course she wanted to see them. She still wasn't sure what she was going to say to them, but yes, she needed to see them.

''I know what you're thinking.'' Joey came up behind her and curled his arms around her, as she stood by the window in the living room staring out at the night lights of the city. "They'll understand, darlin'. They will."

"I wish you had seen them together, Joey. The way Grace made Frank smile. The way they were when they were together reminded me of starry-eyed kids. She's ill, you know, and she can't do the things we all take for granted. Elena has always been there for her, but your father... Frank even brushed her hair." Rhea turned in Joey's arms and laid her head on his hard chest. "I feel so awful for her."

When she looked up at him, he brushed a tear from her scarred eye. "I'm sorry this has been so hard on you." His eyes lowered to the black and blue bruises that roped her neck. Suddenly he set her away from him. "Come on, I'll help you pack. Opal has Nicci's bag put together, and Lucky's anxious to get us in the air." He bent and kissed her lips. "The warm weather and sunshine will do you good. Niccolo, too."

They flew out of a small private airstrip at midnight, and arrived in Key West at four in the morning. When they drove through the gate at Santa Palazzo, the estate was dark and the household asleep, except for the guards patrolling the grounds.

As they stepped from the car, Rhea could hear the surf rushing the beach, smell the salty tang of the ocean. The warm Gulf breeze followed them to the house as they made their way along the paved walkway.

Nicci had fallen asleep on Joey's shoulder in the

car, and as they entered the house, Rhea led him down the hall to Nicci's old room. While Joey put their son to bed, she showed Lucky to one of the guest rooms.

When she stepped back into the hall, Joey was coming out of Nicci's room, and she led him to the bedroom she'd used for the past three years.

She should be tired, but she was too restless to sleep. Joey sprawled out on the bed while she changed her clothes. He fell asleep minutes later, and she slipped out of the room and headed for the veranda.

In the tropical heat she wore a white gauze sundress, and now, as she stood staring out at the ocean, the breeze touched her bare shoulders and lifted the hem of the dress. The predawn sky was clear, and the storm during which she'd departed ten days ago was now no more than a memory.

Rhea left the veranda to stroll along the sandy beach. She was used to seeing guards posted around the estate, and as she passed each one and they nodded to her, she nodded back.

She wanted to be happy, knew that she should be counting her blessings. Joey and Nicci were safe, and Stud was going back to prison. Hopefully the iron bars would hold him this time.

She was anxious to see Elena and Grace, and yet how could she expect them to forgive her for what she'd done? She was responsible for everything that had happened. No, not everything, but the recent situation rested solely on her shoulders. She'd been the catalyst that had resurrected the past and sent Frank to his grave.

The weight of her guilt continued to press down on Rhea as she walked farther down the beach, the balmy night air lifting her blond hair and rustling her weightless dress around her bare calves.

When her sandals filled with sand, she slipped them off and continued toward her favorite spot, where the sand was as level as glass and the sunrise would soon send an orange glow over the Gulf.

Seated on the sandy shore, Rhea tilted her head and let the warm air kiss her cheeks.

It was while she was daydreaming that she heard his voice. At first she thought she'd dreamed it. Then she heard it again, and she turned to see a figure walking toward her.

"*Figlia,* what are you doing way out here? It's the middle of the night. You should be in bed, wrapped in my son's arms."

"Frank?" Rhea scrambled to her feet. "Frank…"

The apparition suddenly stopped twenty yards away, and Rhea once again questioned her sanity, sure he had to be a figment of her imagination.

But then he opened his arms to her and said, "Come, *figlia.* Come see that I am flesh and blood."

"Frank!" Rhea started to run, happy tears blurring her vision. She didn't care. All she cared about was that Frank was alive. Alive!

A foot from him, she tossed herself at the big man

wearing the black eye patch. He caught her and twirled her around and around, saying, "I'm sorry for making you grieve so, *figlia.*"

When he set her feet back on the sand, Rhea looked up into his smiling face. "It was all a lie. Your death…the funeral. Everything."

"Not everything." He turned his head to the side to expose a white gauze bandage on his neck, large enough that it disappeared partly into his shirt. "I did take a bullet. Two, in fact. That wasn't part of the plan—ricocheting bullets. But other than that, Joey's scheme went down just like he planned it.

"Joey?" Rhea wiped at her tears. "Joey arranged your death?"

"Sounds crazy, doesn't it? I thought so, too, when he laid the plan out for me. But it was my only way out, *figlia.* My son knew that. I had to die so that I could live."

"But Joey was shot, too. Did he—"

"That one was no accident. It was vital to the plan to make everything look legit. To make it look like Carlo's men had hit us, blood needed to be spilled. Jackson wasn't happy about it. In fact, he was damn mad. But his marksmanship is the best I've ever seen. Right shoulder, two inches low, one half inch off side. He hit Joey dead center."

Rhea was speechless. Jackson had deliberately shot Joey. They'd planned it….

"With the feds' help and Jackson's connections at the CPD, we were able to get the cooperation we needed to get me out of there, and turn up the heat on Carlo. Lucky flew me back here that same night.''

''And why wasn't I told?'' Suddenly Rhea felt angry that she had been kept in the dark. Yes, she was thrilled that Frank was alive, but she should have been briefed on the plan. She should have been spared the agony she'd been living with for four days.

''I was going to tell you. That is, until you started crying that morning. That's when I knew that your tears would convince the world that Frank was really dead.''

At the sound of Joey's voice, Rhea looked past Frank to see Joey strolling toward them.

''I'm sorry, darlin'. I wanted to tell you. I was going to, after the funeral. Then hell broke loose and changed my plans. Then I thought I would tell you on the plane, but you fell asleep, and again I decided to wait.''

Rhea watched as Frank took a step back and faced Joey. ''It was a damn fine plan, Joey. You'll have to bring me up to speed on what's been happening since I made my final exit from Chicago.'' He turned back and gestured to Rhea's neck and the bruise on her cheek. ''By the looks of that, things turned sour for a while. I want to hear all about it.''

''We'll talk, *mio padre*,'' Joey said, his eyes still fastened on Rhea.

Frank glanced at Rhea once again. ''Go easy on my son, *figlia*. He only did what he had to do.'' He leaned forward and gently kissed her bruised cheek. "We'll celebrate with breakfast on the veranda. Grace will be happy to see you and hold Niccolo. And Elena..." He glanced at Joey. "You will finally meet your sister." Then he turned and started back to the house, whistling.

As they watched him walk away, Joey said, "I've never heard my father whistle."

Rhea turned her gaze on her husband. "Your father always whistles when he walks on the beach."

Joey had never spoken about his feelings for his father, but Rhea suspected that, though there had been rough times, the Masado boys and their father had come full circle.

"I'm sorry, darlin'. You were hurting thinking Frank was gone, and I—"

"You made Jackson shoot you."

"*Si.*"

"That night on the rooftop, you left knowing you would come back shot."

"It was the only way. Jacky's a good shot. Better than good."

"I don't care how good he is—what if something had gone wrong? Frank wasn't supposed to get shot, but he did." Rhea turned away, unable to believe that Joey had gambled so recklessly with his life.

"There was a contract out on Frank. If I could turn the tables and set up Carlo at the same time, then we stood a chance of beating him."

"So you came up with a dangerous plan that could have gotten you killed."

"It was dangerous but—"

Rhea spun around. "You have a son, Joey. A son who loves you and would be devastated if he lost you. You had no right to gamble with your life."

"It's over, darlin'. In Chicago, Frank Masado is dead. Now, as Frank Palazzo, he can live here with Grace without having to keep looking over his shoulder."

"Grace and Elena knew the plan?"

"No. They didn't know anything until Lucky flew Frank back here. But I imagine Frank's told Elena the truth. He said he was going to."

Rhea studied Joey standing in the moonlight. His white shirt had been freed from his jeans. It was unbuttoned, revealing the cross on his neck—a promise to his brother and Jackson that together they were unstoppable. And it appeared they had once again beaten the odds.

She stared at the cross, remembering the night he had slipped it around her neck, then made love to her with such tenderness and care that it had made her cry. That night they had made a child together. And since that night, each and every time she held Nicci, she was reminded of the precious gift that he had given her. That gift, their child, had validated their love.

She had never heard him say the words, but she knew Joey loved her and his son. She'd seen it in the way he held Nicci, and in the way he had looked at her when he rescued her in the motel.

Suddenly it all made sense—why they had flown to Santa Palazzo in the middle of the night.

"Rhea...what's wrong?"

"You're leaving us here, aren't you, Joey."

"Why do you think that?"

"Because I've figured you out. You're Frank's son. The Masado men guard what is theirs. They do whatever they need to, to make that happen. Lucky says when you want something you are unstoppable." Rhea looked him in the eye. "You can forget it, Joey. I'm not staying here."

"Rhea, listen."

"No! I'm not going to let you arrange our lives without asking me what I want."

"I know what you want, darlin'."

"Do you really? You've never asked. How could you possibly know the depth of what I'm feeling?"

"You want Nicci to be safe. Here he will be safe. You told me the first day you came back to Chicago that our son's safety was the most important thing. And I agree. Santa Palazzo is where he needs to be."

"So we stay here and you return to Chicago?"

He looked away. "It's not a perfect plan, but it works."

The silence between them was punctuated by the pounding surf.

"I'll come for visits. We'll live—"

"Like Frank and Grace have for twenty-four years," Rhea finished.

"Survival is everything. We already discussed that."

"Yes, we did. But I no longer feel like I once did."

"What are you saying?"

"I'm saying give me a choice or set me free."

He shook his head. "You have no choice in this matter. You're my wife."

"Take us with you when you leave, or give us up."

"Non posso."

"What can't you do? Take us with...or give us up?"

"Dammit, Rhea!" He took a step forward and reached for her.

Rhea eluded him.

"Come here!"

Instead of doing as he said, she backed into the water.

"You told me this was home."

"I was wrong. Home is where you are. Wherever you are, Joey. I can't go back to living in a dream world. None of us can."

"I can't expect you and my son to live in a cage for the rest of your lives. Nicci needs fresh air and a swing. He needs—"

"His father. And his father can put a swing on the

rooftop. We'll have picnics every Sunday overlooking the city.''

"How could I expect you to live like that?''

"How could you not, knowing we can't live without you?''

Her words made him close his eyes. *"Basta!''*

Rhea shook her head. "No, it is not enough. Not until you are willing to listen.''

His eyes opened and his jaw flexed. "For the last time, Rhea. Come here.''

The wind swirled Rhea's dress around her legs and sent the surf rushing toward her, but she didn't move. When the water engulfed her legs, Joey suddenly reached for her, but again she scurried back farther into the water.

"I'll have the words I know are in your heart, Joey. And then I'll have your promise that it's forever.''

He began stalking her. "You belong to me. My wife. My rules. Here, or in Chicago. I will never let you and Niccolo go, darlin'. I can't.''

"Why, Joey? What's in your heart?'' Rhea taunted, aching to hear the words he had never spoken. Locking her knees as the water rushed them again, she said, "Do you ache for me like I ache for you, Joey?''

"You know I do.''

"Do you wake up anxious for my touch the way I do for yours? Does my touch shatter you the way your tenderness shatters me, Joey?''

"Yes! Damn you, Rhea. Yes!"

"Damn you right back, Joey."

This time when he reached for her, Rhea let him drag her forward. In an instant he was kissing her, crushing her to him. The reckless tide stole Rhea's balance, and Joey followed her down to the water's edge, the waves lapping at them where they lay.

The weight of his body and his aroused need sent Rhea moaning, then pleading, "Let this be our time, Joey. We'll live a day at a time." She gripped his face, spoke the last to his eyes. "And when it is over, my love, we will have no regrets and ask no more. Please, Joey. Take us with you. Take us home."

His hands were in her hair, his eyes moist with unshed tears. "A man would be a fool to refuse you, darlin'."

"You're no fool, Joey."

He bent his head and slowly kissed her, then said, "No, I'm no fool, darlin'. *Ti amo,* my wife. Till death do us part. *Ti amo* forever."

Epilogue

Three days later, six major players in the Chicago-Italian mafia were arrested. It wasn't exactly the feds who were responsible for all the files and records that suddenly appeared on Hank Mallory's desk at the CPD, but just how they had gotten there wasn't mentioned.

All the CPD would release to the media was that the arrests were due to a deep-cover operation the feds had been working on for several months.

Among those arrested were Vincent and Sophia D'Lano, Mickey Norelli, Carmine Solousi, and a number of Carlo Talupa's soldiers.

It was also reported that an unfortunate car accident in the transportation of Stud Williams back to Joliet Prison had resulted in the man's death. No one could explain the bizarre accident, or why no one else was injured. An investigation was ongoing.

Twenty-four hours later, Carlo Talupa's body was found in the back seat of a gray sedan at Ronnie "Crusher" Cardoli's Salvage Yard. He'd been shot six times, execution-style. He was still wearing his felt fedora and the navy-blue coat he'd been seen wearing at Frank Masado's funeral.

Two days later a letter arrived at P.O. Box 720 in Key West, Florida, addressed to Frank Palazzo. The letter clearly stated that the feds were in mop-up mode and that the air in Chicago was beginning to smell sweet again. Definitely, it was cleaner than it had been, and cooler.

The day Lucky flew Joey, Rhea and Niccolo back to Chicago, he got a phone call from Vito Tandi. The call summoned him to Dante Armanno for a meeting to discuss the favor that he and Joey owed.

The favor ended up to be complicated. Lucky wasn't happy about any of it, and he made it known as he relayed his afternoon meeting with Vito to Joey and Rhea that evening at the penthouse.

Snuggled together on the couch in front of the fireplace with Nicci asleep sharing both of their laps, they listened as Lucky ended his story with "CEO of the Tandi Corporation, that's one helluva favor."

Joey studied his brother, thought over Vito's request that Lucky become his heir, then said, "He's pretty specific about what he wants. He's got the details ironed out and…" He hesitated. "He's got a couple of good points, Lucky. Did you talk to Jacky about it?''

"*Si*. He likes the idea. But then, it's not his life that's going to change. Or yours, for that matter.''

"At least you know up front what you're getting into,'' Joey reasoned.

Lucky drained his glass of scotch, then said, "I'm going home and getting drunk.''

"This could be good for us, Lucky.''

"I hear what you're saying, *fratello*.''

"I think you should sleep on it,'' Rhea said softly. "Things always look better in the morning.''

Lucky glanced at Rhea and said to Joey, "Smart lady, your wife.''

Joey eyed Rhea, then his sleeping son, then Rhea again. Her beautiful blue eyes were heavy lidded. It had been a busy day, packing to fly back home. Anxious to get her into bed, he said, "I think going home and sleeping on it is a good idea. We'll talk tomorrow.''

Lucky shoved to his feet, then stepped forward and kissed his sister-in-law's cheek. "Good night, Rhea. I'll call you, Joey, and let you know what I've decided.''

When they were finally alone in front of the fire, Joey said, "I'll put Niccolo to bed with his teddy bear, and then I'll be back to tuck you in.''

"I'll be here. It's been a long day and I'm exhausted.''

Joey slid Niccolo to his shoulder and stood. Looking down at his wife, he said, "How exhausted?"

Rhea smiled, sent her gaze over his body.

"I know that look, darlin'."

With innocent eyes, she asked, "What look is that, Joey?"

"The one that tells me that I should leave a note with Gates to call Opal in early to feed our son breakfast."

"Oh…that look."

"Yeah, that look." Holding Niccolo close, Joey bent forward and kissed her. Then he straightened and offered her his lazy Sicilian smile. "A man would be a fool not to act on that look."

"And as you've already proven to me more than once this week, you're no fool, Joey."

"No, just a man in love."

She stood, stretched like a cat, then purred, "Put our son to bed while I write the note for Norman, Joey. I feel like sleeping until noon. *Capiche?*"

*   *   *   *   *

When it comes to survival,
no one does it better than Lucky Masado.
Don't miss the conclusion to Wendy Rosnau's
BROTHERHOOD *series,*

LAST MAN STANDING,

coming in June from
Silhouette Intimate Moments.

CLAIMING HIS OWN

These men use charm, sex appeal and sheer determination to get what they want—so these women had better be very careful if they have things to hide....

RAGGED RAINBOWS

by *New York Times* bestselling author

LINDA LAEL MILLER

Would Mitch Prescott's reporter instincts uncover *all* of Shay Kendall's painful secrets?

SOMETHING TO HIDE

an original story by

LAURIE PAIGE

Only rancher Travis Dalton could help Alison Harvey— but dare she risk telling him the truth?

Available March 2003 at your favorite retail outlet.

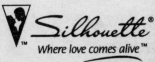

Silhouette®

™ *Where love comes alive*™

Visit Silhouette at www.eHarlequin.com   PSCHO

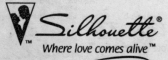

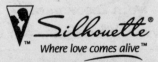

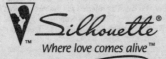

COMING NEXT MONTH